PYRAMIDS

Dolores Storey

Fisher King Publishing

Dedication

There's a darkness in this world
and if you find yourself in the pits of it
use this story as your light.

If I can stop one heart from breaking,
I shall not live in vain.
Emily Dickinson

Special thanks to Victoria, my friend, my
aunt, my second mom. You will be proud to
know I *finally* got this book done.

A note from the author...

Before we get to the story I would love to know who takes the time to actually read Author's Notes. They are only a few pages long and yet they seem to get in the way when the reader just wants to read the book. But alas just to torture you, I shall include one.

Just like most readers, I skip the author's note, I'd think, 'Let's get to the drama, tears and ass kicking!' However, I don't think many writers read author's notes either. Perhaps no one will read this note, but I feel that it has to be written, it's just the done thing.

This story started from my childhood. It was like my destiny. When I was a kid and people asked me what I wanted to be when I grew up, I immediately said, 'an Egyptologist!' Sure, I had plenty of reasons in wanting to become an Egyptologist, more than I could possibly count. But the main reason was simple, I loved ancient Egypt. But my grade school teachers, friends and family saw me differently. They saw me sitting in the corner of the room, at eight years old, reading the works of Edgar Allan Poe and Emily Dickinson. I could recite *The Raven* quicker than my classmates could recite their ABC's.

What I didn't realize at that moment was that I didn't just love Egypt, I loved reading as well. Soon, my English teacher started giving us writing assignments. I blossomed, I didn't know it at the time but I know it now. I knew, ever since I picked up my first book and started to create stories of my own; I knew that I was supposed to be a writer. Most people never know what they want to do with their lives.

Hell, people who have their whole life planned out are still unsure about what they really want. That's why, any time I get a chance to open up my word processor and type out an idea, I feel like I'm living my life.

The idea for this book came to me at the age of twelve. I had just got off of a plane; a cramped one that showed terrible chick flick movies on the backs of seats and served up questionable mashed potatoes. I had just landed in Egypt. Ever since I was a child, it had been my dream to go to Egypt and study their ancient ruins. So you can imagine that arriving at my dream destination was far too much for my twelve year old self to handle. The mass excitement resulted in a stomach ache, most likely caused by those potatoes.

I remember the night air feeling cool and tasting funny, as if it was thick with sand and dust. I found it funny when people said that Egypt was cold at night, but growing up in Michigan, where forty degrees is chilly, the night weather in Egypt was something to look forward to. Every day, I was able to explore ancient tombs that hadn't been seen by humans in years. In one tomb that hadn't been opened in twenty years, I found the inspiration for Pyramids.

My dad was gasping for breath within the tombs and my mom was in danger of getting heat stroke. The guide had helped me down a ladder to see the makeshift burial chamber of this tomb. The tomb itself belonged to a pharaohs musician some five thousand years earlier. It was small and the man's body was behind glass, fitted within the rock. The idea for Pyramids hit me as strong as the thick air. It started with the idea of a young girl visiting the tomb of her friend, a musician. Now this idea had evolved by the time I got back home, it developed from just a tiny scene in my head to something huge, as you will soon see.

Just before my trip to Egypt I lived in Kentucky, USA. Bullied for being 'a Yankee' (since I was born in the *very* northern state of Michigan) I ran away from the brutality of the world and I found a safe haven in a tiny antique shop. There I met the shop owner, a wonderful woman called Diane. She had as much love for Egypt as I had. We would spend hours getting excited over some of the ancient Egyptian objects she had within her store. We were like little kids looking excitedly into the window of a giant toyshop.

Years later and how many states away, she continues to inspire me daily; with every scene, every chapter and every sentence. So this story is also dedicated to her. She was like Obi Wan Kenobi to my Luke Skywalker, only she didn't die in a fight with Darth Vader. She helped me in understanding that everybody needs someone, or something, in their life to make them happy. It doesn't matter if it's a person, a toy collection or a book. We all need a match to light our candles so that we can see through the darkest parts of our lives.

Finally, a story within a story (my favorite). As a kid, I always struggled with depression and anxiety and the only thing that would help me out would be watching movies, specifically Star Wars. Anyone who knows me will understand how important Star Wars is to me; I feel that it saved my life. That's not exactly the point; the point is that I swore to do something for people who are also going through some personal trouble, to give them something that will make them happy. I want this book to work as a torch to guide them out of the difficulties of life. I never wrote to be famous or to get money, I wrote to help people.

This is what I think, people's lives are held together by strings, like a puppet. Every string holds something important, it helps them to fight on. It doesn't matter if you only have just one small thread holding you up, that is a start, something to build on; people need something to hold onto no matter how small. I can only hope that the stories

I write will help you, like so many books, movies and TV shows have helped me.

As I grew older, my tiny aches and pains that came with growing up got worse and soon, walking was even a struggle. This meant that my dream of Egyptology was a no-go, my dream went straight to the dump. No one knew what was wrong with me, why I cried when I had to stand up or how a little slip or fall would put me in bed for a week. I saw no hope... Hell, sometimes I still don't.

But one day, I was sitting in bed as the sun rose, another night spent on editing and trying to get my mind off my pain when I discovered something. It was something I hadn't seen since I had first created this book. I had found hope in my own story. For a moment I was thirteen years old again fighting my way through teenage problems side by side with Astrid. I had found salvation in my own characters' struggles. I thought if they could go through all this, then maybe I could too and that is the greatest thing a person can get from a story. Hope.

Pyramids

Many years ago, on the small Aztec island of Tolico, hundreds of people with extraordinary blue eyes were kidnapped from their native kingdoms and brought to be sacrificed to the Gods.

The inhabitants of this island were themselves imprisoned and living in great fear. If anyone spoke a word about the cruel and heartless actions committed by their leader, the one behind the deaths of the blue-eyed people, they themselves would be killed.

Only one person could bring an end to this insanity; the young princess, Astrid of Egypt. Astrid had been told that she was one of the last people on Earth whose eyes were blue but when faced with a ruthless, barbaric enemy she made a vow to do everything in her power to bring the guilty to justice.

The Princess with the Blue Eyes

The young princess was sleeping peacefully in her bedchamber when she was suddenly woken by the sounds of horns and drums from outside the palace walls. Unsure about the noises she heard, Astrid rose from her bed and looked around her chamber, trying to find something to cover herself. Finding her golden cape near her dresser, she grabbed it and pulled it over her white linen shift. Combing back her hair with her fingers, her body lethargic with sleep, she left her room in search of the source of the noise. With each step she took along the marble hallways, the sound of horns and drums grew louder. She made her way to the large golden doors of the palace. Now fully awake and filled with curiosity, she pushed open the doors and went outside.

People were dancing and singing, filled with cheer and merriment. Not far off from the festivities of the people, Astrid caught sight of her mother and father, the pharaoh and queen of Egypt. The two were sitting upon their mighty thrones, next to a tall, mysterious man who Astrid did not recognize. He wore a large, gold crown which glistened in the sunlight, adorned with dark rubies and from which peacock feathers stood. He wore a white, cotton kilt along with a small pouch, which seemed to hold a knife or dagger. The most peculiar part about this man was the large tattoo on his inner wrist. Not many Egyptians wore tattoos, at least not like this. Its style was unusual, consisting of thick black lines. The design was also peculiar, a single line extending from the wrist, followed by a line cutting across the wrist and a smaller line just below it.

Who is that man? Astrid thought to herself as she walked to her parents side. *Is he the new priest from Karnak? His attire is unusual, I've never seen a priest wear such items. He doesn't look like an ordinary priest. It is almost as though he is not Egyptian.* She was confused, but also curious about who this man could be.

As she got closer to her parents and the mystery man, Astrid was soon standing in front of him.

"Oh my! Are you Princess Astrid, the only princess in all the lands with blue eyes as deep as any ocean?" The tall man asked, with a booming voice that seemed to shake Astrid's entire body.

"Yes sir, I am Princess Astrid, why do you ask?" Astrid said.

Hearing such a response from the young princess, her mother immediately pulled at Astrid's dress and frowned at her.

"Do not ask questions Astrid, especially to our guest." She composed herself, looked up at the man and gently laughed, "I am so sorry, you must understand how children can behave."

The man smiled and said, "I completely understand!" He looked back down at Astrid and she noticed that his smile had changed from being extremely friendly into something that looked quite deranged. "My name is Moha. I am the king of Tolico."

"Oh, I see. What are you doing here in Luxor?" Astrid asked.

"Astrid!" Her mother exclaimed while trying to keep her composure.

"You need not worry your majesty. I myself, have also raised a young girl around her age. I have realized that they are just too young and impatient. They just do not understand royalty like we do." King Moha looked down at Astrid and continued, "Your majesties, I have come to see the princess with the blue eyes."

Astrid was not impressed with this man, even if he is a king. After being treated like an infant, she did not care who he came to see. "Too young to understand royalty? Do you realize who you are speaking to? I may be just fifteen years old but that does not mean I do not understand royalty!" Exclaimed Astrid through gritted teeth. She grudgingly gave a slight curtsy, just to be polite. "Now if you will excuse me, your majesty, I have other important things to attend to," and with that, she spun around on her heels and walked away with her head held high, leaving both her parents and King Moha dumbstruck.

Despite the mighty speech that Astrid had made in front of King Moha, she was still furious at the king's blatant statement about her lack of understanding. "I do not understand royalty... How dare he! Doesn't he know who I am?! I don't even think he is a king. His crown is ridiculous, it looks like a peacock sitting on his head. I can't believe he has the nerve to say such things, acting like he knows everything." Stomping her way to the castle, she pulled the palace doors open whilst continuing with her angry speech about the mysterious king. "I feel sorry for the girl that he raised. Having to live with such a pompous man, acting like he knows everything and he thinks I don't know anything! I know more about royalty then he does and I am just fifteen years of age! I bet he doesn't know that Pharaoh Tutankhamun started ruling at nine years old - oof!"

Being preoccupied with her anger for the King, she remained oblivious as to where she was walking. Storming around the corner to her chamber, she ran right into the temple priest and fell to the marble floor.

"Your majesty! Are you alright? You must always watch where you are going. You could fall right into a hippo's mouth and not even realize it," the priest said as he offered his hand to help her up.

Taking hold of the helping hand, Astrid rose to her feet and brushed herself off, "I am sorry sir, I was just rambling on about... stupid silly things," she sighed.

The priest looked upon the young princess with gentleness. He knew when the princess was feeling troubled. He folded his arms and said, "Well your majesty, it sounds like you need some rest. A young lady such as you shouldn't be concerning herself with such silly things. You must be calm and reasonable as our young princess. Now, off you go."

If only you knew what I had to endure today, then you would be thinking differently, Astrid thought.

After being told to go to her room, Astrid removed her golden cloak and sat on her bed, listening to the world outside and thinking about the people of Egypt. But all that came to mind was the thought of Moha and his stupid crown. There was no way that she could get any rest at this rate. She needed to walk, try to get that damn king out of her mind. She pulled on her cloak and tugged the sheer fabric of the hood over her eyes. The wonderful thing about her cloak was that she could still see through her hood, whilst her eyes remain hidden, making it impossible to recognize her as the blue eyed Princess.

"I will not be punished for speaking my mind, forced into my room like an infant and made to feel sorry for what I said. He should be punished, he was the one who insulted me...", Astrid muttered to herself. Peering outside of her room, Astrid glanced from side to side, making sure that no one was nearby. All was clear, she closed the doors to her chamber and, moving swiftly but quietly, Astrid ran softly down the marble hallways, making sure to land on her toes whilst carrying her shoes. The last thing she wanted was to be caught by the palace guards and then escorted to her room like a child. Finally, she made it to a secret exit that would lead outside without anyone knowing. She put on her shoes, made one more glance around and then left through the secret passageway.

Astrid felt more relaxed, being free to walk through the marketplace and to enjoy the view of the people. As she strolled along the dusty street, she stopped at a wooden cart piled with dried figs and nuts, which had been baked in the hot sun. "How much are they?" Astrid asked the man behind the cart.

The merchant was a stubby old man who peeked up from the cart and stared at Astrid long enough for it to be rude. His unkempt gray beard caused him to scratch at it constantly and his hair, white and wiry completed the disheveled look. He then glared at the fruit for a moment, as if he was totally and utterly confused at what figs were or how he got to the cart in the first place. It looked like the man was completely lost in his own world.

"Sir…?" Astrid repeated.

Finally his eyes were wide open and alert and he started pointing shakily at a group of figs.

"Erm, free! Free for a noble like you miss! Say, you don't already have a husband do you?"

Perhaps it was just the stench of drunkenness on his breath or just his overall nature but Astrid was having none of his nonsense. She gave a slight but irritated smile and shook her head. "You know what? Never mind about the fruit." She reached into her pocket and tossed two gold coins on the cart, "Now go sober up and make yourself more presentable"

So much for feeling relaxed, Astrid thought to herself. After about an hour of strolling around the square, she saw that the sun had begun to set. She knew that she had to return home before it was noticed that she was no longer in her chamber. She walked to the palace and managed to get in without anyone seeing. But as she approached her room, Moha and his awful excuse for a crown were standing next to her bedchamber door.

"Excuse me, your majesty, but men who are disrespectful towards real royalty are not allowed to be near the princess's bedchamber." Astrid said sarcastically.

Moha let out a frustrated sigh, "My apologies your highness. I don't think you understood what I had said earlier. No matter, I wished to speak to you about some… political business."

Astrid frowned, "Oh I understood completely. Now tell me what political business it is of which you speak? I thought you said I was too young to understand politics?" She said mockingly.

The king ignored her remark, his eyes were now displaying much annoyance with the young princess. "Well, let me tell you my theory on the color of your eyes."

Astrid made a gesture to allow the king to continue with his theory.

Moha nodded, "I believe that the gods sleep in your eyes and because of that my people want you to be our princess. If you came with me, to Tolico, we believe that the drought would cease."

Astrid had never heard anything more ridiculous or hilarious in her life. "You think I would leave Egypt, my own kingdom for yours? Ha! What kind of person do you think I am? I would never leave my home. You sir, are a very stupid man, in assuming that I will come with you, based on your theories. Now you and your theories are to leave immediately!" She pushed him away from the door, the surprise of which made him stumble.

"Your highness!"

Astrid growled a curse beneath her breath and muttered, "Yes?"

"You are making a terrible mistake, Princess Astrid."

Astrid turned from the door and cocked her head to the side. "Are you threatening me, your majesty?"

Moha straightened his posture, his deranged smile now stretching from cheek to cheek. "I would never threaten a princess, I only wish to share the message of the gods." He looked up at the ceiling and continued, "If the gods are angry with Tolico and will only be calmed by your grace, then what do you think they will do to Egypt if you did not oblige by their wishes?"

Astrid smiled and turned back to the door, saying loudly, "Well, if the gods wish to punish me for doing my duty as the princess of Egypt, then let them strike me down where I stand." She paused for a moment, waiting with her arms outstretched for something to happen. She then turned her head back to Moha, "Oh well, look at that! I guess the gods do not wish to destroy me", she laughed. "Now Moha, the princess of Egypt must get her rest. I bid you goodnight and farewell." She entered her bedchamber and slammed the door shut, making sure that the got the message loud and clear.

"Ignorant fool..." She mumbled as she put on her linen dress and crawled into bed. Lying beneath the covers she looked down at her feet which just hung over the edge of the bed. She was much taller than the average Egyptian woman and a more recent growth spurt had left her needing a longer bed. This didn't bother her, but what did bother her was what this King Moha said, that she was 'making a terrible mistake.' What did he mean by that...?

In the middle of the night, whilst Astrid slept, the door to her chamber creaked open. Slowly and cautiously, a masked man entered the room and crept to where Astrid lay. Getting closer, Astrid stirred as she heard something above her, the sound of heavy breathing. She slowly woke but still drowsy from sleep the sudden sight of a large shadow cast over her bed alerted her immediately. The perpetrator realized the issue and placed a large gloved hand across her mouth and one around her throat. Astrid kicked and punched with all her might but was easily overpowered. Fear and panic welled up inside her as she struggled but her efforts of escape were to no avail. The attacker dragged her from the bed and pulled her into the hallway.

Astrid was forced onto her knees quickly gagged and in a matter of moments her wrists were skilfully bound with thick rope. Whilst the perpetrator concentrated on his work, Astrid was trying to think of a way out, what could she use or how could she free herself. But she couldn't think, her heartbeat was rapid and she kept gasping for air. Suddenly, in front of her, she saw a pair of worn sandals come into view. Though she had never paid attention to these pair of feet before, something in her head clicked and she recognized them instantly.

The man bent to his knees and took Astrid's jaw in a vice-like grip, tipping her head up and forcing her to look him in the face. "I told you that you were making a terrible mistake princess. But do not worry, we are going to soon solve it, aren't we?"

Moha grinned his demented smile whilst pushing a strand of black hair behind her ear. Astrid struggled, lunged forward and caught his lip with her forehead immediately drawing a small droplet of blood.

He laughed and wiped it away. "I have to give it to you princess, you have much courage. But you are quite arrogant. We'll have to fix that, along with a few other things, won't we?" He dropped her jaw, rose up and gave a short nod to the man behind her. Astrid was nervous even though she fought not to show it, she tried to turn but the man gripped her shoulder firmly.

Suddenly everything about her went hazy and any

strength she had, simply wilted away. Seconds later, she felt everything go black.

The man let out a relaxed sigh, no longer worried about restraining the princess and looked back toward his master.

"Your majesty?" He asked.

Moha crossed his arms and said sternly, "Take her to the boat Acalan, do whatever you want with her, just make sure you keep her alive."

*L*ost

The darkness was slowly subsiding; Astrid was beginning to wake up from her long slumber. She finally came around albeit still groggy, only to find herself in an unfamiliar room. The rigid floor and the cold air struck her body, like a thousand pins pricking the surface of her skin. A feeble attempt at softening the floor with a thin cotton mat, lined with a coarse canvas sheet only made Astrid feel more uncomfortable. Her body felt lethargic and it throbbed with pain, making it hard for Astrid to move. She could only imagine that her restless night was the result of her aches and pains. But when she thought about it, she couldn't actually remember anything that happened after her kidnapping. Her memories merely blurred together, vaguely recalling someone laughing, the strong stench of urine and the sharp smell of chemicals. *It doesn't make any sense* Astrid thought to herself.

Suddenly, she heard noises in the distance, possibly a person, or even a group of people. The sounds of shuffling feet and dishes clanging were vibrating within Astrid's skull. Her head began to throb rapidly with every sharp sound. *Make it stop,* she thought. But she soon realized that she needed to do something, *I can't just sit here, I need to find out where I am and more importantly, how I can escape.*

After summoning up what little strength she could muster from her aching body, she sat up from the coarse mat and reached for her cloak, but it was nowhere to be seen. She stretched her hand out onto the icy marble floor, the cold piercing her palm. She pushed her fingers against the stone and as soon as she looked at her arm, she noticed that it was covered in bruises and scratches. She didn't remember how they got there, but she now felt that she needed to search her body for any more injuries. She sat back on the mat, where a dried puddle of blood stained the center of it along with the lower half of her dress. Astrid swallowed hard, fear seeping into her mind, thinking about how the blood got there and why there was so much. But she couldn't afford to dwell on the matter, she had to do something quickly. Just beside her, there was a basin of water and alongside that lay a thin white dress with a dark blue shawl.

Astrid looked down at her dirty, blood stained dress, the blood had become dry and crusted. She pulled it off over her shoulders and then over her throbbing head. She grabbed the sponge from the basin and began to wipe down her limbs. The water was freezing, causing her body to tense. It felt as if the water was biting every inch that the sponge touched. It also felt odd and worrying for Astrid, washing away blood that may or may not be her own. The blood on her thighs and stomach looked as if it belonged to her, but the more she thought about it, the more worried she became. The fact that she didn't remember her trip here made her worry even more – wherever here was, but she soon began to think about the possible outcomes, an attempt to make herself feel assured. *I could have been kept in a meat cellar for all I know and the blood from the hanging animals may have dripped onto me.*

She placed the blood soaked sponge into the basin and grabbed the white shift. It looked nothing like the dresses she usually wore. This had short sleeves and appeared to be much stiffer. Still, it was better than nothing at all. The dress hid most of the cuts and bruises, but she still felt exposed. So she tied the shawl around her shoulders, covering as much as she could.

Now that Astrid was clean, she needed to consider her options: *Should I start to investigate the noise in the distance? Or stay in this room?* Astrid thought that perhaps safer wasn't always better. She rose on her shaking legs, her body still filled with pain and she made her way to the door, using the wall as support. She swung open the wooden door and was met with the sight of a wide hallway and a stone stairwell. Unarmed and weak, Astrid felt herself already second-guessing her decision, but in spite of the little voice in her head telling her to stay, she continued.

With each step her trembling knees soon became sturdier and stronger. But this was soon replaced with a painful ache as she reached the first platform of the stairwell. She swallowed hard and tried to ignore the pain as she continued walking down the steps. As she reached the bottom of the stairs, she caught a glimpse of a small kitchen.

"Is anybody there?" She called out as she stepped into the small space. Empty. That's strange, where are the cooks she thought. Suddenly, a short old woman came around the corner. She's too old to be working. And why is she by herself? Before Astrid saw anything else, she noticed how cold the woman's gray eyes were, filled with such sadness that Astrid had never seen in a person before. Her eyes made her almost look like a corpse.

In noticing Astrid, the woman quickly brushed some white powder off of her brown dress and swung a long gray braid of hair behind her back. With a gentle curtsy she said, "Your highness!"

Astrid suddenly felt extremely exposed. Something about the old woman scared Astrid, yet she somehow felt comforted. But not enough. "Am I supposed to know you miss?" Astrid muttered, pulling her shawl over her shoulders.

The old woman gasped and quickly curtsied again,

"Oh! Oh, no your highness! I am but a servant. My name is Xoco, I am the cook."

Astrid had never heard such an unusual name before.

The woman turned back to a set of chairs surrounding a small table all simply carved from wood, "Please m'lady, sit down! You look awfully tired".

Astrid willingly let Xoco lead her to the table and into a seat, even though she remained unsure about the woman.

"I've made you some atole, I'm sure you're starving!" She placed a steaming bowl in front of Astrid. Warmth, something Astrid gladly welcomed. She sat down at the table and handed Astrid a wooden spoon. Astrid looked down at the pile of mush that resembled something a bit like porridge, but worse.

Despite the welcoming warmth radiating from the bowl, she didn't feel very hungry. She nudged the bowl toward the center of the table. *I need answers.* "I wish to know the price of my ransom. Do you know it? My family are extremely wealthy so they will pay any price for my freedom." Astrid proudly stated whilst straightening her sore shoulders.

Xoco looked surprised, "Oh no child, why would you have a ransom? You haven't been kidnapped; didn't you volunteer to come here?"

What kind of story had Moha told this woman? Astrid looked down at her bruised hands and gritted her teeth, "I was taken from my slumber, there was no permission or volunteering in any way, shape, or form." She looked up, took in a deep breath and calmly said, "Now, please tell me that wherever I am has some type of herbs for pain relief. My trip has not been a pleasurable one and I am not even certain about how I got half of these bruises."

Xoco's smile quickly faded. She gave a nod and slowly rose from the chair.

"Yes, I have something that may help," Xoco said as she

went in haste to find her lotions and potions. She opened a cupboard and reached for a large vase. Suddenly, something furry and gray let out a high pitch shriek and leapt from behind the container. Xoco yelled, almost dropping the vase and the animal jumped onto the table. Astrid pushed herself away from it, in fear that it was some cursed spirit. But it was far from being a cursed spirit. It was a scruffy, gray kitten, which looked just as frightened as Xoco did. Astrid let out a relaxed sigh and moved back to the table.

"It's just a cat." She said, scooping up the kitten and holding it gently in her arms. The kitten coughed and then hacked up something from its throat. Xoco grabbed a piece of cloth and placed the kitten onto it.

The cat gave a final gag before Xoco screamed again, "Dear gods!" Xoco gasped, stumbling away from the table. Astrid had never seen anyone so terrified of a cat. She looked down at the kitten, which was now licking at his paw. She gently shoved the kitten aside before looking at the vomit, thinking that perhaps Xoco was frightened at the sight of a regurgitated mouse.

But in place of a half-digested rodent was a small blue pendant. Astrid picked it up, wiping the lapis stone with the cloth she inspected it closely. For being in a cat's stomach, it wasn't in bad shape. It was actually quite pretty. It was shaped like a teardrop and hung from the remains of a makeshift chain. Astrid was beginning to wonder how it had gotten into the kitten's stomach in the first place.

Astrid looked back at Xoco, who was beginning to calm down.

"Don't worry, the cat isn't possessed," Astrid said, "He coughed up a necklace, that's all. Continue with what you were doing if you can." Xoco shuffled back to the cupboard while Astrid calmed the kitten. She had to admit that the cat helped take her mind off her pain. A few moments later, Xoco returned with a small bowl of herbs. She sat down beside Astrid and handed her a thin piece of cord.

"I don't think this is going to help my pain," Astrid muttered, taking it from her.

Xoco laughed and said, "It's for the pendant. I'm getting something for you right now…" Something in her voice had changed. It seemed unsettled. She set down the bowl of herbs and spooned them into a cup of water, "This should help your pain your majesty. Though… you should see a priest. The gods may be angry with you and are causing you pain…"

Astrid slowly took the cup from Xoco, trying to hide her confusion of how the gods could hurt a kidnapped princess.

"It wasn't any god, it was obviously my kidnapper. What kind of gods would hurt a victim?"

Realizing that Astrid had a good point, she quickly diverted the discussion toward the kitten, saying, "You should name the cat, but the king doesn't approve of animals within the house, so you had better conceal it." Xoco nervously looked down at her hands and tried not to look back up at Astrid.

Astrid thought for a moment and considered the name Nefert might be good for a cat but she had more pressing things to worry about. As she mused she threaded the pendant onto the cord that Xoco had provided.

"Xoco!" Yelled a sharp voice that echoed throughout the kitchen. Xoco quickly took the kitten and walked outside, hiding it from sight. A moment later, King Moha walked in and stood in front of the stone table. Before he could see the necklace, Astrid had quickly slipped it around her neck and covered the pendant in the neckline of her dress.

"Good morning, Princess Astrid. How was your sleep?" He asked.

"Fine… it was much better, compared to last night when some king with a stupid, obnoxious crown and some masked man took me from my kingdom and dragged me into captivity," Astrid answered sternly.

"Good... then Xoco will take you outside for a tour of your new kingdom," the king said.

"Oh, how delightful. Because that's all I want to do", Astrid muttered sarcastically as she rose from the table.

Astrid headed toward the door but Moha, now glaring at her, blocked her path. "You are a stubborn little brat, but don't you worry my dear, this little game you're playing, in being such an obnoxious thing... you will soon lose," the king whispered, before returning upstairs.

Despite his sinister statement, Astrid remained undeterred. After Moha left, Xoco gave Astrid a thin rope that was tied to Nefert's collar, to use as a leash.

"Thank you, Xoco," Astrid said.

"Here m'lady, try this," Xoco suggested as she took a small brown square from the pocket of her cotton shift. Astrid took the object from the old woman and looked at it with curiosity. "Eat it, it's good for you," Xoco said happily.

Astrid took a small bite from the corner of the square and gave Xoco a little smile, "What is it?" She asked as she took another bite.

"It is a sweet nourishment that will keep you going," said Xoco. Astrid had never tasted anything as sweet and smooth before.

When they reached the outside of the house, Astrid realized that the building they had been in stood alone. It looked bleak and feeble when compared to the palace. The walls were practically falling apart and dominated by a thick wild climbing bush. Astrid wasn't surprised that the king was keeping her in a cold little house. As they walked further into the square, Xoco told Astrid more about the Aztec delicacy that she was eating. While they strolled, Astrid saw a large, brightly-colored, step pyramid, glimmering in the sun. On top, many people were chanting louder and louder around a person hanging by their feet from a tall pole.

"What are they doing Xoco?" She asked. She was curious about their chanting. But suddenly, the chanting stopped and one man came forward and spoke in a language which Astrid did not understand.

In realizing what was happening, Xoco quickly turned Astrid's head away from the scene and then there was silence.

"We need to go now," she whispered as she pulled Astrid's hood up over her eyes and tugged at Nefert's rope. They quickly headed back to the house.

Xoco opened the door, and tightly grabbing Astrid's arm, said, "That was a bad thing you almost saw, it could happen to you!" Astrid was surprised but nodded in agreement. It was then that Astrid noticed that Xoco's storm-gray eyes had turned even darker. Something was not right.

"Go up to your bedchamber and do not look outside, do you hear me child?" Xoco said sternly as she pushed Astrid toward the stairs.

As she climbed the cold steps to the bedchamber, King Moha stood in her way. Astrid noticed that his hands were covered in a thick, crimson colored substance and the blade of his obsidian dagger, which was strapped to his side, was also covered in a crimson substance, staining his kilt with a dark circle.

"Ah just the princess I wanted to see," the king said.

Astrid frowned, "Oh, just the king I did not want to see," she grumbled as she pushed him away and continued to her bedchamber. As she reached the top of the stairwell approaching the small room where she had earlier woken, she noticed another room across the hall, its door slightly ajar. She looked around, to make sure King Moha had not followed her. Astrid slowly opened the door; there was a large sleeping mat and a wardrobe with a stand where a crown would usually sit. The walls were decorated with a complex Aztec design.

"This must be where King Moha sleeps," she whispered to herself. She entered the room, knowing full well what the king was capable of and what he would do to her if she were caught. Despite that, she walked over to a large gold chest encrusted with rubies and sapphires. This room looked nothing like the others and she wondered why the king sleeps here when he has the palace, perhaps it was to keep an eye on his prisoners. Casting her thoughts aside, she inspected the gold chest. As she opened it, a small painting which hung above the chest, fell to the floor,

"What's this?" But just as she spoke, she heard footsteps approaching. She quickly picked up the painting and ran to her bedchamber.

"Princess Astrid?" Called Xoco.

"Yes?" Astrid answered.

Xoco smiled and walked into her bedchamber, "I did not mean to be so rude but I needed you to leave. What you almost saw was a human sacrifice to our gods; the king thinks that this will convince the gods to help our kingdom."

But Astrid was even more confused than before, "Why would you kill someone and think that would help to restore your kingdom? The ruler is meant to keep matters in order, not to hope for the best by sacrificing people."

Xoco knew Astrid was right and patted her on the shoulder as she left the room.

Astrid grabbed the painting from under her mat. It was old, the paint had faded, but Astrid could make out a young girl around her own age with long brown hair, wearing a short cotton dress and dozens of blue and green necklaces. Though the paint had faded, Astrid could see that the girl had blue eyes and was wearing a blue teardrop necklace. She has blue eyes like mine, and I thought I was the only one, Astrid considered to herself. She wondered who this girl might be and whether or not she may still be alive.

Astrid gazed at the painting in amazement, knowing that there is another girl with eyes as blue hers.

After a while, she carefully placed it under the mat and then walked down the stairwell, "Xoco?" Astrid called out.

"Yes m'lady," she replied in response.

Astrid sat in the wooden chair and looked at Xoco, "Do you think there is anyone else out there like me?" She asked.

"What do you mean Princess?" Xoco answered as she took a seat beside her.

"Someone with blue eyes." Astrid wondered if Xoco would tell her about the painting or not.

Xoco thought for a moment and then answered her nervously, "No, never. You Astrid, are the only one who has blue eyes, always will be." Intercepting the conversation, Nefert meowed loudly.

Astrid knew that something was wrong, but it would have to wait for another conversation. "Oh, well thank you for telling me the truth Xoco, I appreciate that." Astrid stood, gathered up Nefert and said, "Good night," as she went to her bedchamber.

"I don't believe her; she knows something about why I am here and about that girl in the painting." Astrid mumbled to herself. She looked down at Nefert who rested his head on Astrid's leg and purred softly. "You're so helpful little one. But what's more important than that painting is me getting out of here and going home." She laid her head back on a thin, coarse pillow, which had not been in the room when she arrived but it didn't make it any more comfortable. Astrid closed her eyes, trying not to bother herself with the many mysteries of this place.

In her dream, she was in a boat, floating along a glowing blue river. People were talking in the distance, their voices muffled and unclear. But she was able to hear one distinctive voice amongst the crowd.

I don't need to hear details Acalan, she'll be dead soon and those pretty blue eyes will be in a jar.

Astrid was soon awoken by the warmth of the sun on her face, along with the soft purring of Nefert, curled up at her side. "Was that a dream?" She muttered. It didn't feel like it, something about it was far too real and it made her chest tighten with worry.

"Princess Astrid," the king said loudly. She stood up, forgetting where she was for a moment and opened the door slowly.

"What could you possibly want?" She replied.

"Stop acting like a child, people will now be assuming that you are my daughter. So treat me with respect!" He shouted.

"I will not treat you with any respect at all! You are a coward who kidnaps girls and gets someone else to do the dirty work for you." Astrid ran down the stairs and into the kitchen. "Xoco, I need to speak with you please." She said. The small old woman was sitting on a dining chair, eating atole.

"Yes dear, what do you need?" Xoco asked. But they were interrupted by the thunderous footsteps of King Moha.

"You need to talk some sense into that child!" King Moha screamed at Xoco.

"Now calm down your highness, what is wrong?"

"She calls me a coward and treats me with no respect! You need to teach her some manners before I knock her into oblivion."

"I will not treat this man like my father. It's ridiculous!" Astrid exclaimed.

Before King Moha could strike Astrid, Xoco pulled the king aside and spoke to him in a calming tone. Astrid was surprised to see that the cook had such control over the king. She's only a servant. When Xoco had finished speaking, King Moha marched out of the room. He was definitely calmer.

"Now, may I speak with you my dear?" She asked Astrid as she sat down, "The king is having a coronation for you since you are the new princess," Xoco explained.

"The new princess? What makes you think I'm going to willingly be coordinated? Where's the old princess?"

I wonder who the old princess was, Astrid thought to herself. *King Moha said he had raised a girl my age before, so then, why can't she be the princess?*

Xoco was trying to think of an explanation for the missing girl and after a few seconds she replied nervously, "She um... grew up and married a poor man and died a very, very long time ago."

Astrid did not believe her for a moment. But she told Xoco that she would go to the celebration, in order to prevent any discourse. She also wished for her dress and hood to be washed and hemmed, she needed to look presentable, even for her own coronation.

Xoco laughed at her and said, "I will get a cotton shift for you to wear until I am done with your clothes."

When Xoco returned, she brought a cotton dress with a deep-blue headscarf. "Here you are, my dear."

Astrid took the clothes and went up to her bedchamber to change. Astrid pulled the dress over her head and tied the headscarf around her hair. The dress was identical to the girl's dress in the painting; it hung to her knees and had small pleats along its length. Astrid was happy with the look of it and walked down the stairwell.

"Oh you look beautiful!" Xoco exclaimed. She ran over to Astrid and hugged her, "Just beautiful!"

For a cook, Xoco appeared to care a lot for the wellbeing

of Astrid.

While Astrid was waiting for her dress to be finished, she decided to go for a walk. Astrid strolled along the dirt road, her hand brushing against the palace wall. Once again, along the lake, Ra was about to enter the netherworld. Even though the lake was enchanting, reflecting the majesty of the sun within its ripples, fear had flooded her mind. Worry sunk into her chest, she still had no plan of how to get back to Egypt. Even if she ran away right now, there was no way for her to get home and she would be caught and brought back to King Moha. This walk was making her feel more fearful.

"Xoco? Is my dress finished yet?" Astrid asked as she turned the corner to see Xoco, seated next to the riverbank and quietly washing Astrid's dress.

"Hello my child," Xoco said as she turned away from her work. She stood and held the dress up to Astrid, "It was heavily stained and your hood had a hole here and there, but it was easy to fix. I don't know how blood got on it though."

Astrid was delighted to see her dress looking as good as new. "Are you coming with me to the coronation?" Astrid asked as the two walked back to the house.

"Maybe." Xoco said, pulling open the door of her home.

"I do not speak the language that some of the people speak, how am I supposed to talk to people or answer the questions they ask me?" Astrid did not want to look a fool in front dozens of people. To be honest, she didn't really care for learning the language, but she thought that Moha or Xoco might suspect her plans of escape if she remained quiet during the coronation.

Xoco thought for a moment and said, "I will ask the king for permission to help you, alright?"

Astrid nodded and took her dress from Xoco before running up to her bedchamber to change. When she was finished, she put on her sandals and braided her hair while Nefert purred against her leg.

While she usually had her own servants to braid her hair, she knew how to do it. "My father always told me to have a plan... but I don't have one yet," Astrid muttered. "They say the god Baset takes the form of a cat and protects the people of Egypt. Did you come to help me Nefert? Give me a sign Baset, use this cat as your vessel and tell me how to get home."

"Are you finished changing yet?" She heard Xoco ask from outside the room. Astrid opened the door and Nefert ran out, meowing loudly. "The king wishes to speak to you, he is in the kitchen," Xoco said.

"Alright." Astrid said. She wondered if he suspected something. Or what if he knew that Astrid had taken the painting of the young girl from his room? The idea made her chest tighten with anxiety.

"Princess Astrid, I want to talk to you before we leave." King Moha said, adjusting a gauntlet at his wrist, not bothering to look up at Astrid as she entered the room.

"What else do you want?" She snapped as she crossed her arms.

"I don't want you to say anything to anyone unless they ask you something and I expect you to answer without the attitude, do you understand me?" Moha growled, looking up from his wrist.

Astrid gritted her teeth and with a fake smile said, "Perfectly clear."

The Art of Surprise

Preparing herself mentally for whatever was awaiting her on the other side, Astrid walked into the large ballroom, the marble floor gleamed brightly and the walls were adorned with Aztec murals of their gods, looking mighty and fierce. Seeing all of the people, the decorations and the hall itself reminded Astrid about her home in Egypt.

As far as she could see, there were hundreds of people shimmering from the jewelry and colors that they wore. The women wore many beaded necklaces that covered their bare chest, each one possessing an intricate pattern. Their arms were covered in colorful bangles, their skirts were adorned with many beautiful jewels and colors and their headdresses were covered with such colorful feathers and gold that they looked like exotic birds, waiting to be admired and loved. Similarly, the men wore extravagant headdresses which were adorned with gold, their kilts were also golden, glimmering like the sun and their arms were also covered with bangles, but not as many as the women. Despite everything that had happened to her, Astrid was amazed at the culture and attire of the people of Tolico, how their embellishments made them appear powerful. But, the idea that this place was even close to resembling anything in Egypt made Astrid feel incredibly nervous.

"What is wrong?" Xoco asked.

"Umm... there are just a lot of people here. I'm just a bit overwhelmed." Astrid lied. Just moments away from her coronation and she still had no plan of escape.

Xoco smiled at Astrid, placing her hand gently on her

shoulder and said, "It'll be alright child, I promise. There is no need to worry."

That's only making me feel worse... Astrid thought.

"Astrid, come with me. I want to introduce you to someone," King Moha said to Astrid, dragging her away from Xoco.

Taken from the only person who treated her with kindness, Astrid began to worry, a cold shiver ran down her spine. But she couldn't afford to show any sense of weakness in front of King Moha, she needed to remain strong. The two walked through the crowds, most of them staring at the young princess and whispering eagerly to each other. Then, in the distance, she saw a short old man sitting in a chair and talking to a small group of men. After realizing that they were approaching this man, Astrid's stomach dropped. She was in no mood to have a conversation with an old, seedy man.

"Cacama, it has been quite some time since the two us last spoke." King Moha said whilst eagerly shaking the man's hand. The two started a casual conversation, almost forgetting that Astrid was right there.

"Oh, where are my manners! I almost forgot. Please, meet the new princess, her name is Astrid."

Cacama laughed and gave Astrid a good, long look, as if he were inspecting a camel for sale. Looking satisfied at what he had seen, he said in a low tone, "Well, hello there dear." He gave a sly grin, as if to give Astrid the impression that he was charming.

"She is unlike any other princess," King Moha said with a grin and continued, "she's quite special and I think you may like her."

"Well, King Moha, go ahead and show me something special. I see nothing special with this princess." Cacama gave another look at Astrid, this time, focusing on her breasts. "Nothing at all." Astrid shifted uncomfortably and adjusted her cloak in order to prevent his gaze.

"Take a look at her eyes Cacama, they're as blue as the ocean. You can't tell me that those aren't special. And even if she is lacking in a few things, they'll soon come through. She's still young." Moha said with an eager laugh, gripping Astrid's shoulder firmly.

Cacama let out a deep, hearty laugh. "That's true, that's true! I bet that you'll become a very fine queen one day," he said, winking at Astrid. "Perhaps a good wife as well, eh?"

His snide remarks were grating on Astrid's last nerve. She clenched her jaw tightly, wanting nothing more than to punch Cacama square in the face.

As much as the thought of seeing him try to speak with a broken jaw, instead, she calmly said, "Just because I'm young and pretty, doesn't automatically mean that I'd be a good queen or a good wife. A person should be judged by their merits, not on their appearance. I can be whatever I wish to be because I'm independent and intelligent. And I do not tolerate filthy pigs who leer at me like I'm an animal for sale."-

Cacama laughed at her. Astrid was surprised that he found that funny. "She's got spunk Moha, I'll give you that. But you'll need to tone it down somehow."

"Oh I will, believe me." Moha chuckled, whilst giving Astrid a stern glare.

"Beg your pardon sire, but Astrid needs to get ready for the coronation," Xoco announced from behind, resting her palm on the center of Astrid's back. She whispered to Astrid, "Come Astrid, let the men continue with their business."

As Xoco ushered Astrid away, she resisted for a moment and said in a stern voice to the men, "Before I leave, I would like to state that I am not an object, nor is any other woman. So you should start treating women like people, not like a pretty bird trapped in a cage."-

Leaving them speechless, Xoco immediately pulled Astrid away, grabbing her arm a bit too tight, "Come on dear, leave it be." Xoco whispered whilst she ushered Astrid outside of the grand hall, leading her down the hallway and through a passageway that led to the house.

They went into Xoco's room, where she had everything prepared for Astrid.

"Now m'lady, just sit here and we will get started." Xoco said whilst preparing her brushes. Astrid preferred it when her servants added elements to her face, she was not used to the wobbly hand of Xoco. Afraid that she would poke her eye out, she started fidgeting.

"Please stay still Astrid. You're making it difficult for me to apply the powder to your eyes." Xoco said.

"Well, if your hand wasn't trembling so much, perhaps I could." Astrid snapped. Xoco paused for a moment, her face looking sad. Astrid became confused and worried.

I didn't mean to upset her. She asked Xoco, "What's wrong? Ever since we entered the hall, you've been acting differently, as if something is worrying you."

"My apologies m'lady. You know how coronations are, they can be quite stressful." Xoco said. Astrid wasn't convinced. Something is bothering her. Before Astrid could ask her any more questions, they were interrupted by a forceful knock on the door. She was worried that the door would break down with such force.

"Why are you taking so long? You should be done by now." King Moha said as he barged into the room. He looked at Xoco, giving her a long, grim glare before pulling Astrid away from the safety of the room, towards a set of large golden door. She could hear people behind the doors, their voices muffled and low. Then it grew louder, and they were beginning to cheer and applaud as a pair of guards grabbed the handles of the doors and pulled them open.

This isn't the same hall that we were in a moment ago,

Astrid thought. Astrid's heart began pounding rapidly, feeling that it would break free from her chest. She suddenly felt extremely claustrophobic. There were so many people surrounding her and there was no way out, the guards were stationed at every door, keeping Astrid trapped.

"Sit," the king demanded. Too fearful to speak back, Astrid sat as instructed, in a large golden throne, which looked much like the one she had at home. The king began chanting something in a foreign language.

She swallowed hard and looked towards the main doors. She thought of running from this throne, diving into the ocean of people and to charge toward the doors. The thought of running out into the cool night air, to keep on running until she reached home filled her mind. The thought of running into her parents' arms, to hug them tightly and never let go, to hear them say, 'We love you' and to finally know that everything would be fine. Coming back to the loud chanting, she immediately thought of the moment on top of the stepped pyramid, how they were getting ready.

Oh no, oh no, please no! Tears began to stream down her face. She closed her eyes and placed her hand on her chest, praying to the gods that she will be saved. *Please... Save me!*

"Wait!" Yelled a voice from the distance. Astrid turned to see Xoco standing behind the crowd and in between the golden doors. Amidst the violent chanting, she heard Xoco's voice so clearly.

"Astrid run! Run now or he will kill you!"

This was her opportunity. King Moha looked preoccupied with Xoco. She had to run. Before she even stood up, a group of guards were charging towards the podium they were standing on. She had to make a break for it. This was different now, it wasn't just about getting home, this was a matter of life or death. Feeling the King's glare digging into her skull, she broke into a run and rushed into the crowd. Some began to scream, others tried to grab at her, she could feel their nails dig into her skin. They began to yell more, their screams getting louder and louder. The more they yelled, the more Astrid ran.

She could see the main doors but the guards now stood in front of them. There was no other option, no other way to escape. She kept running, thinking that she could run straight through them. She didn't care if they killed her, she would have at least fought for her life and not die at the hand of Moha.

The doors were getting closer and closer, the guards unsheathed their swords, ready to strike her down. Astrid closed her eyes and thought back to her home. She thought of her bed, the way her feet would hang off the ends, the way the sun looked at midday and how the soft warm sand felt between her toes. What she would do to be there one last time.

Suddenly, she felt the doors against her palms. The guards were writhing in pain and they were scattered amongst the howling crowd.-

How did that happen? They should have struck me down...

Despite her amazement at the guards, she needed to move quickly. Running through the hallways, she searched desperately for a way out. Astrid looked around, terrified at deciding which route to take. She tried to remember the route that Xoco had taken which led to the house. Trusting her intuition, she ran straight along the hallway.

Please let there be a passageway, please! Just then, as if by the power of prayer she caught sight of the passageway. *Thank the gods!* She ran on, wasting no time looking back. As soon as she reached the kitchen, she ran through the door that led to her freedom. She felt the cool air hit her face. She looked for a place to hide before the guards came after her, but the only thing in sight was a giant barrel, probably for wine. Sitting next to it were a more barrels and a couple more just across the dirt road. Even if it is filled with wine, it was better to drown than to be caught. Anyway Astrid knew she could hold her breath for a little while but begged to the Gods that the guards would net get thirsty.

The Girl of the Forest

She was hesitant about choosing a barrel that sat on the edge of a hill. But she couldn't be picky. With limited choice, she reluctantly grabbed the lid and stepped into the barrel. Luckily, it was empty. She saw a small hole in between two panels. Peeking through it, she just barely managed to see the barrel squashed next to hers. No wonder the barrels were sitting out on the side of the road, these were filled with holes.

Astrid sat on the bottom of the barrel and started to poke her finger through the crack. *What am I going to do now?* She thought to herself hopelessly. She didn't know how to get home or if there was anyone that she could trust. She cursed under her breath and sighed. Suddenly, her finger hit something in the other barrel. Whatever she hit, it let out a yelp and it knocked the barrel against Astrid's. Both of the barrels quickly tipped over and fell backwards, causing them to roll down the large hill.

It felt like all of her bones were being rattled about. Finally, the two barrels crashed against a rock and broke open. Astrid was lying on the grass, her limbs now covered in new bruises and the air knocked out of her lungs. Just above Astrid, a figure was standing near her head. Astrid thought that someone had come to take her again. But as she gulped for air the moonlight shone on the figure, the light revealed it was a young girl, roughly about Astrid's age. The girl kneeled over Astrid with a confused and concerned expression on her face.

"Are you OK?" She whispered, brushing back her short

black hair.

Feeling confused, Astrid nodded and slowly sat upright. Her body was aching, but she tried to shrug it off.

"I assume you were the one who poked my back?" The girl asked while folding her arms. She started to shiver from the cold night air, but she remained composed while she interrogated Astrid. "That was quite rude of you," the girl said.

Astrid furrowed her brows and backed away from the girl, "I'm the rude one? Who do you think you are?"

The girl growled something under her breath, trying to look as intimidating as she could in front of a stranger.

She blew at her bangs that covered her eyes and scowled at Astrid. "My name is Hitomi, I was once the princess of Japan. Now, who do you think you are?"

Astrid cocked her head to the side. She wasn't sure that she liked this girl's attitude. Of course, she would never admit that she would have acted in the same manner.-

"My name is Astrid. I have been the princess of Egypt for the last fifteen years and I will not be ordered around by a child."

Hitomi laughed and said, "I'm the child? You said you have only seen the last fifteen years. Yet I am the child. Do not act like you have authority over me when we are practically the same age".

Astrid was ready to yell at Hitomi but Hitomi had already gone up the hill to search the area. Once she had returned to Astrid, they could see dozens of torches being lit in the distance yet close enough that the two girls could hear men speaking amongst each other.

"We can finish this argument later," she muttered to Astrid. "I can only imagine that they're looking for you. And the only way you managed to get this far was by escaping. You said you were a princess of Egypt, yes?" Astrid nodded.

"Then come with me your highness, I've got a place to hide."

Hitomi led Astrid deeper into the forest, occasionally looking back to make sure she was still following. Finally Hitomi stopped, she turned toward Astrid and stretched out her hand. "Take it in yours, I can't have you getting lost."

Astrid was hesitant but she took it, she had never trekked through a forest before and could easily get lost. Hitomi continued to lead her deeper among the trees. With the occasional sound of dried leaves and twigs crushed beneath their feet, the silence between the two girls was almost deafening. Astrid wanted to break the silence; she needed to know more about this princess anyway.

"You said you too are a princess? How did you get here? Why were you hiding?" Astrid asked as she stepped over a thick branch.

"I was taken when I was five years old. The king of this island has no wife and was unable to be blessed with a child of his own, so he stole someone else's... me. My mother and father were killed by Moha during my kidnapping. I assume my uncle is now the king of Japan, but it doesn't matter. For all he knows, I am as good as dead, just like my parents. I was meant to be a sacrifice to the gods that Moha worships. When I was brought here, his servant didn't believe it was right to sacrifice a five-year-old, it might make the gods angry. So they kept me hidden for two more years but then I was able to escape. I've been living in the forest for the last four years. The guards are afraid to come here because of the animals. But they're just cowards. I mean, I've been out here for years and I haven't come across anything yet. You'd think they would at least try to find me."-

Hitomi looked over her shoulder at Astrid and winked, "But I am pretty good, if I do say so myself. I hunt my own food and everything; those guards would be dead within a few minutes, I'm sure. They're just fools who get angry without their wine."

Astrid didn't know what to make of Hitomi's willingness to speak about her kidnapping. But her story reminded Astrid of her own ordeal, and she had to wonder if she would have been sacrificed on that throne, just as Hitomi was meant to be slain.

"Well!" Hitomi said as they reached a small clearing, "Home sweet home!" Then Astrid saw it. An old, worn and forgotten shack covered in thick brush.

"There's food and water inside, though there's only one cot so you'll have to sleep on some gathered leaves." Hitomi continued as they approached the shack. She wiggled the door handle and pushed it open.

The inside wasn't as bad as the outside. The cracks in the walls had been patched up with thick brush and there was even a working fireplace. The small cot was made from long, woven blades of grass that had been braided together, with a basin next to it. Astrid had to admit that Hitomi had done pretty well, considering she had been living by herself in the wild. But it was still surprising that this girl had survived in the forest for so long, able to fend and to forage for herself. Astrid thought about the notion of being lost in the woods, how would she have coped without anyone else to help her.

"Sit down I'll get you…" Hitomi paused. Something had caught her attention. She glared at the fireplace, where a small gray kitten lay sleeping on a grass rug.

"Oh what the hell?" She growled, marching over to the cat. Astrid immediately recognized the kitten and ran to stop Hitomi, who had now armed herself with a sharp spear.

"No! I know that cat!" Astrid yelled. "It was in the palace where I was held captive." She reached inside the neckline of her dress and pulled out the teardrop shaped pendant, "He gave me this!"

Hitomi froze and dropped the spear. Her eyes looked down at her chest where an identical pendant hung around her neck, attached by a worn strip of twine. Hitomi slowly looked up, with a look of shock on her face. Then they both realized something very surprising about each other.

Astrid clamped her hands over her mouth in an effort to silence a scream. The light from the dimming fire illuminated both of their faces, making their eyes shine. Astrid could see bright blue eyes staring back at her. In that moment, they both saw something that they thought was impossible.

Before either of the girls could utter a word, a crowd of people back in town began to yell and chant. Their voices could be heard from the deepest part of the forest.

"Oh this is bad, this is really, really bad." Hitomi muttered and cupped her hands over her ears.

"What?" Astrid asked.

Hitomi paced the room, mumbling something in a different language.

"What are you saying?" Yelled Astrid.

"Anata wa yagi no o shiri de okasa rete kita!" She barked, running over to a large chest in the corner of the shack.

Astrid stared at Hitomi in confusion. "What did you just say to me?" Astrid growled, "What was that?"

"You're screwed Astrid! They're looking for you!" Hitomi yelled before pulling out a long silver sword.

Astrid slowly backed away, hoping Hitomi wasn't planning on killing anyone. "What are you going to do with that?" She muttered. Hitomi closed the chest lid and glared back at Astrid.

"They're looking for you, ma nuke. It doesn't matter if it's a drunken idiot, I can deal with them! But I can't deal with Moha's army. I need to watch out for myself!"

"Where did you get it…?" Astrid asked in a worrying tone.

Hitomi almost seemed insulted and in reaction, she snapped at Astrid, "How do you think I got this shack?" Astrid thought of the worst case scenario.-

"You killed someone for it?"

Hitomi barked out a laugh, "Ha! Gods no! The man had drunk himself to death. I buried the corpse and took his shack. I found the sword within the chest. Don't think I haven't used this blade though onnanoko. A girl has to get fed somehow." She walked past Astrid and looked through a cloudy window. "We should be fine. You can stay here if you want. Personally, I don't think you could survive out here on your own and honestly," she turned her head towards Astrid, "I have got too much of a heart to let a *little girl* go off into the woods on her little lonesome. Now go to sleep, I've seen the house Moha keeps his captives in and it's uncomfortable as hell." She nodded towards Nefert. "Take the cat too. You can have my cot tonight, I'll be fine."

Astrid slowly nodded; she slid from the wall and sat on the thick grass cot. Hitomi lay down a few feet away using the grass rug as a pillow.

Astrid lay on her back and stared at the ceiling. She didn't think she had ever been this confused in her entire life. Her situation had become so complicated, she couldn't think about it for more than a moment before getting a headache.

"Thank you for taking me in…" Astrid muttered, looking over at Hitomi.

"Listen," Hitomi said, rolling on her side to face Astrid, "I don't know why you have blue eyes, or how you got away or how you're going to get back to Egypt – I know you're thinking about it – but you shouldn't worry about that now, it won't do you any good. So… you're welcome. Now go to sleep, you're going to need it."

Astrid nodded; she turned away from Hitomi and looked back to Nefert, who was blinking sleepily at her. She noticed something tucked under the furry kitten, something Astrid hadn't seen before. She reached for it and pushed Nefert away. This piece of worn paper had been folded a good seven or eight times and seemed to take forever for Astrid to unfold. But when she finally opened it, an extremely familiar image stared back at her. It was the painting Astrid had found just days before. *How did it get here? Did Nefert bring it?* She sat the painting down and stared at the cat. Perhaps the goddess Baset had heard Astrid and had sent Nefert to bring her home to Egypt.

Even if Baset wasn't watching over her, Astrid was still very happy that she had found Hitomi.

In the Shadows

Waking up to the sight of Nefert sleeping peacefully near her face, Astrid had almost forgotten that Hitomi had helped her hide. It was definitely better to have a change in scenery from the dreary house that she was kept in. Astrid's drowsiness was suddenly awakened by the smell of something cooking.

"It's nice having some company, been awhile since I've spoken to someone although cooking for two is a chore," Hitomi said as she walked from the fireplace. "But it's fine." She said she sat next to Astrid and handed her a small wooden bowl filled with steaming soup.

"So, as we're getting to know each other, how did you get the name Astrid? It is pretty kudaranai if you ask me."

Astrid didn't know what to make of the foreign phrases that Hitomi occasionally spoke. She assumed that Hitomi thought of her name as being... odd. Astrid was a bit bemused by such a statement.

"What's wrong with my name?" Astrid muttered after taking a spoonful of soup.

Hitomi shrugged and crossed her legs beneath her. "Nothing I guess," she said as she sipped her broth. "It's just weird."

"My father named me after a rare blue flower that can be found in the middle of the desert. He said, 'Only people who are blessed by the gods have the pleasure of seeing the Astrid.' He said that instead of giving him a flower, the gods blessed him with a daughter, me. A seer foretold that the gods would give him a son of silver swords. But instead, he got a daughter of blue flowers." Astrid said, pushing around a piece of corn in the bowl. "So, I don't think it's weird." Astrid whispered.

Suddenly she became silent. She didn't want to talk about the origin of her name, or about her father. The thought of home had made her feel sad, she longed to return to Egypt and be rid of this place.

"Oh, well that is really interesting. Definitely not a weird name anymore. I wish that my name was as special as yours. I don't think anyone explained the meaning of my name to me. Maybe they would have told me when I was older... But I do remember my mother calling me Hana." Hitomi paused and looked into her bowl of soup, her eyes looking lost and confused. "I'm not as lucky as you Astrid. I can't remember what my home was like, what my parents may have told me or what they even look like... I feel so lost at times."

The strong independent girl who led Astrid through the dark forest disappeared. All Astrid could see at this moment was a lost little girl who was frightened.

After a while, Hitomi chuckled and stood up from the floor, returning back to her original self.

"Anyway, you don't have to be shy with me when talking about your home. And if you don't feel like talking, that's also fine. I understand. But I'd like to think that I'm far better company than King Moha." Hitomi laughed whilst putting her bowl away. She then looked over at Astrid and squinted her eyes. "So, I assume you were taught how to fight, unless the women of Egypt are like the ones in Tolico who are all taught to cook and clean while the men are warriors and live real lives."

Astrid had never felt more confused and embarrassed at the same time. She simply remained silent as she didn't know how to respond.

"I see. Well then, has anyone ever taught you how to

hold a spear, or a sword? Because you're going to need to learn quickly." Hitomi rolled her eyes and went to the large chest to retrieve the sword concealed within. "Moha will be looking for you and he's going to keep searching for a few more weeks at least. The drunk who built this shack chose the perfect place for it to stay concealed within the forest and we can hear any loud noises or sacrifices going on in town, which will give us enough of a warning if Moha is on his way."

Right on cue, the sounds of horses trotting along the dirt roads echoed within the forest and rattled in Astrid's ears.

"Right on schedule. When I escaped, he kept this tawagoto up for a week or so. Even though I managed to keep myself hidden from him, it was pretty hard to even think about leaving this shack since the entire island knew me. Judging from the way you act and the unhealed bruises on your limbs, I guess that you've only been here a few days. That also means the only people here who knew you ever existed are the people who attended your coronation."

Astrid looked up in surprise and asked her, "How did you know that it was my coronation?"

Hitomi gritted her teeth, spun her sword around her wrist and said, "You have to be kidding me, I know what building you came from, I know what's going on and you're still surprised. I'm not an idiot."

Astrid stood and looked out of the clouded window.

"Alright I'm sorry. But, how do you know Moha won't look for me here in the forest? And to answer your previous question. Yes, I have been trained. You know, I have answered nearly all of your questions and you are yet to answer my questions." Astrid said looking over at Hitomi. "What are those weird words you keep saying?"

"One of the only things I remember from my native language, curses. Are you even surprised, Astrid? You shouldn't be." Hitomi rolled her eyes and leaned her sword against the wall. "Now, if you plan on living here with me, you're going to have to do a lot more than make me laugh and talking in your sleep. I don't need the tawagoto. I've got enough food for the day and it's not safe to go hunting with Moha running his wild goose chase. So we'll go get some water since I'm nearly out, is that alright?" Astrid nodded and picked up her cloak from the cot she had slept on the night before. She wrapped it over her shoulders and covered her arms, suddenly feeling as though she needed to conceal her bruised wrists.

"Even though you look like you can't defend yourself, I'll let you stay. But remember Astrid, out here, royalty doesn't exist and there are no servants waiting on you. People don't care if your blood is pure or not, they only care if you'll make an easy target. What's a princess without her kingdom? Nothing, that's what. So you'll have to get used to it." Hitomi barked and grabbed a large wooden bucket by the door. "Now come on."

Astrid nodded in an effort to avoid an argument and secured her cloak before taking a final look out of the smeared window. Just as she did, she saw a figure wobbling through the forest, holding a large basket.

"Um... I think we have an issue..." Astrid muttered as she tried to reach Hitomi.

Hitomi scoffed, "Already?"

"I'm pretty sure - well, I am sure - that someone's coming... Thought it would be important to mention it."

Hitomi spun around, throwing the bucket on the floor she reached for her sword, rushed across the room and pushed Astrid out of the way, in order to keep her hidden. A look of regret flashed across her face, but it didn't last long, Astrid understood that. Hitomi had no reason to give Astrid respect, and Astrid realized that she should stop expecting the royal treatment. Hitomi was right, what is a princess without her kingdom?

Hitomi pushed her face against the window, in the hope that she could spot the intruder before they got any closer. Her guarded nature ceased instantly. She dropped the sword and rushed to the door, throwing it open, and jumping into the arms of a short old woman who had dropped three large baskets.

"Xoco! How are you? I haven't seen you in thirty suns, I was beginning to think the worst." Astrid stepped back towards the wall, bemused and petrified.

Xoco? How did Xoco know where Hitomi was? Was Moha here?

Suddenly, Astrid felt extremely unsafe. What if this was all a trap to get her back to Moha? After Hitomi and Xoco had spoken, the two shuffled inside and sat the woven baskets on the floor beside the fireplace. Xoco brushed dust from her dress and turned away from Hitomi. The moment she saw Astrid, Xoco's jaw hung slack, her eyes doubling in size and her hands dropped to her sides.

Finally, after a moment, she clamped her palms over her mouth and screamed, "Astrid!" She rushed over to Astrid and embraced her tightly, "I was so worried about you! Oh thank the Gods, you're safe! You're safe and sound!"

Astrid patted Xoco's back nervously. It seemed Xoco had the strength of a hundred Egyptian soldiers by how tightly she was hugging Astrid, she was afraid that she might snap in two. However, there was something comforting about Xoco's inhumanly tough grasp, it reminded Astrid of her mother's embrace. She let herself slip from her tense position for a moment, allowing Xoco to hold her in a loving embrace.

"You two know each other?" Hitomi huffed looking bemused by the thought.

"Of course, my apologies," Xoco said, finally letting go of Astrid, "I took care of her during the few days that she was at the palace, Hitomi." She looked back at Astrid and said, "I was afraid something had happened to you! It's such a relief to see you safe and sound."

"How did you find me?" Astrid muttered, slowly stepping away from the others.

Xoco clamped her hand over her mouth and shot a serious look at Hitomi, "You haven't told her?" She exclaimed.

"Oh, you're one to talk! She just got here last night, I didn't get a chance!" Hitomi yelled back. It was like a glaring competition between the two.

"Tell me what?" Astrid said, glancing at the two of them, "What's going on?"

Being put on the spot, Xoco composed herself and explained her role along with Hitomi's.

"King Moha has a fixation on people with blue eyes, like you two. He brings them over to Tolico to... I help the captive people escape from Moha when I can, Hitomi was one of the children I saved. I come down here whenever the king is out, to give Hitomi supplies that she may need." Said Xoco, a hint of a proud smile gleaming on her face.

"So, there have been others, you've saved other people Moha kidnapped?" Astrid asked eagerly whilst trying to hide her excitement. If Xoco had saved other people, maybe there was a way Astrid could return home.

However, Astrid's excitement was short lived. Xoco's smile faded and any look of happiness on Hitomi's face vanished as well.

"What? What is it?" Astrid yelled, "Where are the others that you've saved?"

Xoco looked at Astrid, her eyes filled with a lost sense of hope, "It's hard to save everyone..."

Astrid's heart sank.

"Are you telling me they're all dead? Every one?" Xoco let out a heavy breath and looked down at the floor, too ashamed to look at Astrid.

"Are they?" Astrid barked.

"Yes." Hitomi muttered, walking forward and placing her hand on Xoco's shoulder. "Xoco can only do so much for them. Some people are just too weak; they can't live on their own or find a place to survive. Sometimes Moha... He'll kill them before the scheduled sacrifice."

Astrid's heart sank further.

"Why? Why would he do something like that? Who could be that cruel?"

Xoco took a deep breath and said, "He's insane Astrid. He kills these people with no remorse. Adults and children." Her lips curled in disgust, too sickened to speak further. She began to cry, unable to hide her sorrow. Hitomi grabbed a shawl from the cot and wrapped it around her shoulders.

"He eats them," Hitomi explained. "Unfortunately, it's actually quite common in Tolico for the kings to eat the hearts of their sacrifices. But Moha doesn't do that. He squishes the heart beneath his feet, treating the heart as being something feeble. He focuses on eating their eyes. He believes that he can absorb some god-like ability from the eyes. I don't know if he's ever succeeded in gaining special powers from it but I know that he'll do anything to eat someone's pretty blue eyes. There have been tales of the eyes being the source to immortality, which could explain his obsession with beating death. But through his barbarity, the people of Tolico have turned a blind eye to his actions, allowing him to continue with his cruelty in order to avoid his wrath. Considering how many people Moha has killed, it seems likely that we are the only two people in this realm with blue eyes. Which is why Moha has been searching frantically for you. We have to stay in the forest, it's the only place in all of Tolico that he will not dare to enter."

Hitomi quickly turned and picked up two large buckets beside the fireplace.

"Now that Astrid knows more about the island and about

us, we need to act quickly. Astrid and I need to fetch some water and Xoco, you need to return to the palace before Moha is done searching for the day and realizes that you're gone."

Their trek toward the riverbank within the forest seemed to last longer than expected. Throughout Hitomi remained silent, which made the walk a bit tense, leaving the various sounds of the forest to break the silence. Once they arrived at the river, they wasted no time in filling their buckets with the cool water. In realizing that they had time to spare, Hitomi decided that it would be fine for them both to bathe. Astrid was excited at the thought of cleaning herself, it seemed like it had been a while since she had last washed. But even the duration of bathing was silent on Hitomi's part. Clearly she had a lot on her mind to deal with, not least of which was worrying about Moha and his plans.

Astrid stood in the center of the shallow river, letting her body enjoy the warmth of the stream. She watched the minnows swim around her toes, they shimmered beautifully in the sunlight. She had to admit that she was somewhat comforted by the display of the glowing fish. It distracted her from the difficulties of her current situation, allowing her a moment to mentally and physically relax.

They're so innocent, she thought. They had no idea what was going on around them, they were living in an entirely different world and they were happy.

Astrid pushed herself onto her back and floated on the surface of the water, staring at the tree line in front of her. She enjoyed the feeling of her body supported by the water, it felt like she was flying. The cool liquid also helped to sooth any aches she had left in her body.

However, something was peculiar about the far side of the forest. Something seemed so unnatural about it. Astrid became curious, wondering if anything lived on that side.

"Hitomi?" Astrid called out, assuming that she wouldn't hear a reply. She was right. She sighed and whilst she was floating on the water, she rolled her eyes back towards her forehead as far as possible in an effort to see Hitomi.

"Hitomi, have you been on that side of the forest?"

"I can't say that I have. Why?" Hitomi growled.

Astrid leaned turned onto her front and swam further into the river. "There's something uncanny about it. Can you come see…" Something caught her attention, something bright and blue in the distance. She cocked her head to the side and did her best to take a better look at it. Her view was obstructed by a large tree.

"What's going on?" Hitomi asked, swimming over alongside Astrid. "What are you staring at?" Astrid grabbed Hitomi's shoulders and pulled her head to the side, hoping that perhaps Hitomi could see what Astrid could.

"Look there, do you see it? It looks like stone, doesn't it?" Astrid said pointing towards the anomaly.

Hitomi's eyes narrowed, trying to get a good look at the distant object. Her expression was mixed between confusion and curiosity.-

"Can we go see what it is?" Astrid asked. Trying to judge the time of day from the sun, Hitomi knew that they had plenty of time before they needed to return.

Slowly, Hitomi nodded and she turned to Astrid, "Fine, fine. We can go take a look, but you have to understand that it might not be safe over there. There are many strange things in these woods. Xoco has told me that there was a civilization here before Tolico and they were just as crazy as Moha. They might not be around anymore, but their belongings still remain. I don't want to get caught in any ancient spells."

The girls rinsed out their clothes and put on their sandals before heading into the forest. It didn't take long for the sun to dry their garments. Astrid did her best to lead the way towards the glimpse of the blue stone she had seen, but it seemed to disappear and reappear with every step she took.

They suddenly came face to face with a tall wall of wild brush intermingled with trees. It was almost as tall as a pyramid and just as thick as one. For once, Astrid was the first to make a move.

"I'm sure we can make it, we just need to squeeze through the gaps."

"Are you sure that's a good idea? I mean, someone obviously didn't want anyone to get through to the other side of this." Hitomi muttered as she placed her hand against a thick branch.

If only I could move it somehow, Astrid thought. She gave a light push against the branch, thinking that it would miraculously move.

"I have a feeling that your method is not going to work." Hitomi teased.

Astrid sighed and looked beside her to see how far the wall reached, she couldn't see an end to it. She let out a heavy sigh and in a fit of frustration, she slammed her fist against the barrier. Suddenly, the wall of vegetation shook beneath her hand and the thick branch wiggled and fell backwards.

"Watch out!" Hitomi yelled, shoving Astrid away from the wall. In a giant cloud of dust, the structure came tumbling down with the noise of a thousand horses.

"Hitomi!" Astrid yelled, reaching out through the dust.

"It's fine! I'm right here! I'm right next to you!" Hitomi called back. "How did you do that?"

"I hit the right branch I guess..." Astrid muttered, coughing into the neck of her dress, her eyes watering from the dust, which then stuck to her cheeks like mud. No matter how hard she tried to wipe the dirt away, it seemed to become more attached.

Finally, after a few minutes, the dust started to clear,

leaving a huge pile of ruins and rubble from the once great wall. The girls spent the next few seconds looking at each other in a state of shock and horror.

"You have the strength of a god, Astrid." Hitomi remarked, rubbing the dirt from Astrid's face.

"I doubt that, this wall was old, it was bound to break. It's a coincidence that it fell when I touched it."

How ironic, Astrid thought, *the one person who doesn't believe in coincidences and now they use it as a valid explanation.*

"I don't really care what it was. It was strange, that's all I know." Hitomi muttered, brushing the remaining dust off of her dress.

After the girls had enough time to catch their breath, they looked ahead to see what the wall had been covering. Dust still cloaked the area like a morning fog, but both of them knew there was something lurking just behind it. As the dust began to fade, they were able to see a vague outline of a mysterious stone.

Sprouting from the mossy ground stood a colossal lapis pyramid, mimicking the limestone pyramids that stood tall in Egypt. Both the girls fell completely silent, their gaze captured by the mesmerizing glow from the building in front of them.

"I...it's a p-pyramid," Astrid eventually stuttered in shock. "It's a pyramid like back home!"

The Lapis Pyramid

Both of the girls stared at the pyramid for a while, their faces masked with astonishment.

Breaking the silence, Hitomi abruptly asked whilst gaping, "Wait, you know what this is? This... strange block?"

Realizing that Hitomi was left in the dark, Astrid began to explain.

"Back home in Egypt, the pharaohs used to be buried in these tombs. These pyramids represent the glory of the ancient pharaohs and queens of Egypt, being buried with their valuable treasures." Astrid said in a low tone, taking a step towards the pyramid. Suddenly, Astrid was struck with a thought, "If there is a pyramid here in Tolico, that could mean that Tolico and Egypt are connected! I could find a way to go home!"

Hitomi rolled her eyes and crossed her arms over her chest, thinking that Astrid was getting too eager. She then said in a sarcastic tone, "Too bad there's no entrance into this big block."

Astrid was feeling too hopeful now to acknowledge Hitomi's pessimistic tone. In a cheerful tone, Astrid said, "There is though! You just can't see it. The architects made the entrances invisible; there are multiple entrances that are connected to false halls in order to confuse grave robbers. Fortunately, my father took me inside a pyramid when I was younger. No one is supposed to know how to enter one. But I am positive that I can find a way inside!"

Hitomi on the other hand didn't look too happy,

remaining hopeless about the whole situation. She kicked a twig off her foot and in startling Astrid, she started to shove her towards the lapis pyramid whilst growling out a curse.

"Fine, if you can find a way in, go right ahead. But I'm staying here. There's no way I'm going to be cursed by going into one of those things!" She then stood her ground giving Astrid and the pyramid a lethal glare.

"Oh come on Hitomi!" Scoffed Astrid, "A curse wouldn't hurt us, this pyramid is obviously Egyptian and let us not forget that I'm an Egyptian princess!"

"Yeah, and I'm probably nothing to them. *You* might be saved, but I'll be left for dead! Waiting to be eaten by an Egyptian demon or something!"

Astrid sighed and began walking towards the pyramid, saying back to Hitomi, "Have it your way then Hitomi. You can stay here and wait for me to return. I'm not sure how long it will take though so you might be waiting for a long time."

She looked back at Hitomi to see if her expression had changed, she saw that Hitomi remained headstrong in her decision in waiting. Trying to think of something that would make Hitomi change her mind, Astrid finally said, "Oh, I forgot to mention that there might have been something following us back in the forest. Maybe a large animal?" She peered back at Hitomi, noticing that she was slowly beginning to panic whilst trying to remain composed. Astrid continued, "I didn't want to say anything because we were having such a nice time bathing in the river. Then I completely forgot. But I'm sure it won't come out now."

Hitomi began to look around anxiously, wondering if the beast was going to jump out at her. Trying to remain confident, Hitomi yelled out to Astrid, "You can't scare me! You think I'm scared of the forest, I've lived here my whole life! So do your worst!"

Astrid simply shrugged her shoulders and started to

make her way toward the lapis pyramid and putting some distance between Hitomi and herself. Hitomi on the other hand was getting twitchy, her mind telling her to go with Astrid rather than staying out here. She suddenly realized that she has never stayed outside when it got darker, and the sun was getting lower and lower with every second. *If that beast comes out and she finds out about it, she'll never let me live it down,* she thought to herself.

With fear being the victor in this situation, she started to hurry over to Astrid, yelling out to her, "Wait! I've decided to come with you!" In getting closer to Astrid and slowly panting from the running, she continued, "It wouldn't really be fair to let you go in by yourself. You don't even have a weapon to defend yourself. And Xoco would kill me if she knew that I let you go somewhere by yourself."

Astrid smiled at Hitomi, glad that she was coming but she was also secretly proud of herself in managing to make her believe in 'the beast'.

But Hitomi quickly added, "But if I get cursed and eaten by some ancient demon, I'll haunt you forever!"

Astrid laughed under her breath and said, "Alright."

Staring at the pyramid and inspecting every area of its glowing blue surface, Astrid did her best to remember how her father had found the entrance to the pyramid they had been to. There was something extremely different between Egyptian pyramids and this; while the pyramids back home were made brick by brick, this pyramid consisted of huge solid pieces of lapis. No lines, no cracks, nothing that indicated a way in. Astrid's hope began to fade and her frustration grew. It seemed like any time she came close to finding a way home, it was destroyed right in front of her. Astrid let out a heavy breath and sat down on the ground, resting her head on the slick stone.

"There's no way in... its pointless." She muttered,

burying her head in her hands. Hitomi sighed and sat down beside Astrid, placing a hand on her shoulder.

"Are you sure?" She asked with a hint of hopefulness in her voice. Hitomi had thought that if there was a way for Astrid to get home, then there may have been a possibility for Hitomi to get home as well.

Suddenly, everything that Astrid had kept hidden came flooding out. All of her emotions from when she was taken from her home began to engulf her mind. She screamed into her hands and began pounding her fists on the ground. "Damn it!" She yelled, "Gods damn it!" Astrid swallowed hard and squeezed her eyes shut to prevent herself from crying, but it didn't work. Tears starting to stream down her face. She slowly muttered to herself, "I just want to go home…"

Hitomi sighed, knowing she couldn't avoid the situation anymore. It'd been years since she had thought about finding a way back to Japan. She didn't even care to look anymore. She had given up, knowing her fate was to stay in the forest for the rest of her life. And for a long time she had accepted that. She knew that the Japan she wanted to return to was gone, her family was dead and her people had moved on and forgotten about her. But she was alright with that.

However, she never imagined that she would have to see someone else enduring the same agony that she experienced as a child. A part of her wanted to leave Astrid here in the forest, to avoid the issue completely and to go home before the sun went down. But she couldn't, she couldn't leave Astrid here. Hitomi remembered all the times she had wished someone to be by her side as a child when she was homesick.

At that moment, she thought to herself, *Since no one was there for me, I guess the least I can do is be here for her now.*

Hitomi leaned over and placed her hand around Astrid's shoulders. She stared at the blue pyramid blankly, wondering why it was even created.

Who would make a huge structure just to stare at? Everything had a purpose didn't it? She shoved her foot up against the slick stone and started to push at it, thinking that somehow she would be able to move it. Nothing happened, no surprise there. She scanned the pyramid from top to bottom, side to side until she was back to the base, just a single sheet of lapis lazuli.

Then, out of the corner of her eye Hitomi noticed something. On the ground, buried beneath some moss lay an oddly shaped black stone. She moved away from Astrid and started to dig around the corners of it in an effort to get it out.

"What are you doing?" Astrid asked.

Hitomi scooted forwards and started to dig her fingers in deeper into the dirt and under the stone. She was fully immersed in her digging task.

"I want to see what this is." She said, yanking something upwards against the rock. The dirt and moss gave way and suddenly a rock emerged from the ground.

Hitomi started removing the moss from the stone, curious about what it could be. The moss started to peel off like a thick web. Freeing it from the moss, it appeared to be a very unusual stone, one that Hitomi had never seen before. She had never seen a stone of this shape and even though the dirt and mud still kept the rock's surface hidden, Hitomi knew that this rock was not shaped naturally. Someone had put it here.

"What do you think this is?" Hitomi asked, handing over the rock to Astrid. Astrid was hesitant to take it and her hands shook as they groped the stone. Her fingers began to become familiar with the strange object

"I think I know what this is." She said, brushing her

hand at the surface. "It looks just like a stele. Back home, we have steles which depict a set of events on stone. Some of them are drawings, others are written down but they all describe different stories." Hitomi looked surprised. She went up on her knees and spat into the hem of her dress before rubbing at the stone, trying to remove as much dirt as she could.

Slowly, the dirt began to fade and a carving began to take shape. It was as large as the stone itself and appeared to be some sort of symbol. The image depicted a triangle with an oblong teardrop set within it. There were also two vertical lines in the center of the triangle along with a horizontal line at the center of the triangle.

"What is it?" Hitomi muttered as she nudged Astrid's shoulder. Astrid was trying to figure out how this piece could be connected with the lapis pyramid. But this symbol was a mystery to her. If Astrid knew what this pyramid might be, maybe she knew what this symbol was as well, however she did not. Even though Astrid's native written language consisted of many shapes and images, she had never seen this symbol before.

Astrid just shook her head at Hitomi and said, "I've never seen it before in my whole life.

Wait, Astrid thought. There's something about it that looked so familiar, as if she had seen it before in Egypt. She glanced up at the pyramid just as Ra's hot rays hit the blue stone. Suddenly, it became very clear to her. Set into the whole pyramid, barely visible without the sunlight was the stele symbol. Hitomi knelt forward to where the stone had lain in the ground and she started to dig at the edges of the pyramid. The pyramid seemed to be set in deeper than Hitomi had expected. Finally, after digging deeper and deeper into the dirt, her fingers felt a sharp edge.

"Wait!" Astrid barked, jumping forward at Hitomi's hand. "What is that?" Astrid asked as she pointed to two clots of damp dirt that stuck oddly to the pyramid. Hitomi grabbed at the odd pieces of dirt and tried to pull it away. Instead, her fingers fell through the mud and into a small hole in the pyramid. She pulled her fingers out and started to clear away the dirt from the holes.

Once the mud was gone, two shapes appeared in its place. They mimicked the symbol on the stele but the teardrop shapes in these symbols were indented, as if a key should be placed within it. Astrid went down on her knees, looking closely at the indented shape of the teardrop. Suddenly, a weight grew heavy around her neck. She glanced down at her chest and saw her necklace dangling around her neck, as if it was being drawn towards the symbol.

Hitomi glanced at Astrid and saw her pendant, causing her to look at her own pendant, which also seemed to be drawn towards the symbol. She grabbed hold of it and tightened her grip. Both of them stared at the pendant for a while, something about it catching their attention. In unison, both of their eyes widened as they reached the same thought and they looked back at the symbol. Both of their pendants had matched perfectly to the teardrop shape in the pyramid.

Astrid hastily pulled her necklace from around her neck and slipped the pendant into the symbol. Something beneath her hand and the pendant shook but stopped after a moment.

"Is this supposed to be happening? Is this what it does in Egypt?" Hitomi asked, her eyes doubling in size in fear of what might happen. Astrid just shook her head, temporarily mute from shock. Hitomi acknowledged this and instead of asking any more questions, she sat down and quickly pulled off her own necklace and placed the pendant in the matching shape beside Astrid's.

The surface of the pyramid began to shake beneath their hands but this time, it didn't stop. The violent vibrations began to move from their hands and traveled upwards a meter or so, where the trembling got more intense and began to make a vicious growling sound, as if the pyramid was going to crumble altogether.

The smooth surface of the pyramid began to change, the lapis suddenly splitting into different sections. Both of them could hear the blue surface snapping and cracking. The lapis covering the front of the pyramid began to crease and fold, revealing limestone beneath along with a large entrance that was adorned with complex carvings along the sides. The lapis had managed to fold and alter itself into two long columns that stood tall on either side of the pyramid, looking identical to the Egyptian obelisks. There was something about that sudden transformation which was both amazing yet terrifying; the entire act looked like something only a God could create.

"I have a feeling that what happened just now, doesn't usually happen with Egyptian pyramids…" Hitomi whispered.

Astrid slowly shook her head in agreement and said, "No, no I can't say that it does."

The Gatekeeper

"I want to go inside." Astrid whispered eagerly to Hitomi as she stepped in front of the two limestone doors against the pyramid. She could only imagine what was inside, waiting to be discovered.

Before she got any closer to the doors, Hitomi grabbed her shoulder and said, "Whoa whoa. Aren't you at all a little bit freaked out about what just happened? This pyramid somehow transformed! Whoever built this must be keeping something hidden from anyone who comes near it. But I assume that you don't even care, right?"

Astrid stared at Hitomi with a simple smile that showed she wanted nothing more than to go inside.

"Of course... Well I guess I can't say that I am a bit curious. We did after all spend the last hour trying to get into it. Guess there's no going back now." Hitomi began to relax and became more curious about what was hidden within this pyramid.

She playfully shoved Astrid towards the doors and excitedly said, "I didn't just dirty myself like a pig in the mud for nothing!"

Astrid looked back at the door and placed her hands on it. She could feel the dust shift beneath her palms, the roughness of the limestone remaining strong. With a deep breath, she pushed at the door with all her might. Not moving an inch from her force, she looked at Hitomi for some assistance, embarrassed that she wasn't able to move it with a single push. With a smile creeping upon her face, Hitomi came and began to push against the ancient doors.

As they shoved it forward, the doors began to slowly part with a loud deafening creak. They were soon wide open, revealing the darkness within the mysterious pyramid.

The sun's rays worked its way through the trees and into the dark hallway, but the light had only managed to illuminate a small section of the hallway. Astrid knew it wasn't a good idea to go inside. The light only went in about three maybe four feet, beyond that it was pitch black and anything could be lurking in its depths. Even with all of her doubts about the darkness, Astrid looked over at Hitomi and grinned.

Greeting her with a smile as well, Hitomi let out a sigh and said, "Well? Are we going?" Astrid took in a deep breath and nodded before walking into the dark hallway.

The first few meters weren't as dark as Astrid had expected. Even though she thought that the sun wouldn't be able to light the majority of the hallway, it had managed to bring in enough light for them both to see the walls covered in webs and dust. The sun had also illuminated the dust lingering in the air, the tiny particles floating around and making it appear like the starry night sky.

However, the sunlight began to fade and leave them behind as they moved into the depths of the pyramid, leaving Astrid and Hitomi in complete darkness. They both began to rest their hand on the walls as a guide forward amidst the blackness.

"No torches?" Hitomi muttered, glancing back and forth to what she assumed were the walls.

"I doubt it; I don't think this place has been occupied in hundreds of years." Astrid said crossing her arms over her chest. It seemed to be getting colder as they went in deeper into the darkness. Was it ever this cold in the pyramids in Egypt?

They continued to walk forward, despite their lack of sight within the dark. They were no longer able to feel the walls beside them, Astrid immediately assumed that they had reached a hall. As the darkness began to consume them both, Astrid was soon unable to see her own hands in front of her face.

But then, a light began to glow in the distance. Soon a bright blue light began to flood the space they were in, with no torches in sight. The girls exchanged a look of confusion and stopped dead in their tracks. They didn't ask each other where the light came from. Instead, they just stared at each other with the same look of bewilderment.

Finally, something caught Astrid's eye. She looked up at the ceiling to find the light source. Hundreds of glowing particles lit up the ceiling like stars. Astrid had never seen anything so beautiful in her entire life. It was like this pyramid had ensnared the night sky itself.

"What are those things?" Astrid whispered, tapping Hitomi's shoulder.

"They look like the tears of the gods." Hitomi gasped.

"I can assure you, those are not the tears of gods, just keys," came a deep voice from the distance. Suddenly, the unlit torches burst into flames around a figure who was now encircled by the luminous fire.

"I was hoping that the two of you would find your way here." He said with relief, in a deep gruff voice.

Astrid felt vulnerable in the presence of this man, not knowing what he could do or how had he been waiting for them to arrive. Acting on instinct, she clenched her fingers into tiny fists, preparing herself for the worst. She looked over at Hitomi who had already positioned herself into a battle stance. They were both ready for a fight.

As he stepped forward, the man crossed his arms and simply smiled at them both.

"Welcome. My name is Tacama. I am the Gatekeeper. I had sent a cat after one of you with the key to the pyramid. I had to conceal the key within the cat in order to prevent it from being taken. For a moment, I got worried that he had lost his way. But seeing you both here, I am glad that you have managed to find your way." His smile grew, probably happy that he had some company at last. "How is he by the way? The cat?" He asked out of curiosity.

"Nefert? He's fine." Astrid answered, wondering if Nefert belonged to this man.

He laughed gently at the name, happy that the kitten had found a home. He then offered his hand toward the girls, as if waiting for one of them to take it. "Now, will you both join me inside?"

Hitomi stepped back and raised her fists, dubious about his intentions.

"Before we go anywhere with you, we want answers first. So, who are you? What is this place?" She commanded.

Tacama paused, looking quite puzzled at Hitomi's authority and his arms dropped to his side. "As I have just stated before you ladies, my name is Tacama and I am the gatekeeper. 'This place' is the Tolico pyramid and I keep it safe from crooks and trespassers. I've been trying to get the attention of you two girls for quite a while now. It's nice to meet you both." He folded one arm around his back, the other over his front and he bowed.

Hitomi glared at Astrid with frustration. But Astrid couldn't help but to marvel at the stranger's strong sense of etiquette.

Upon seeing Hitomi's reluctance to trust the gatekeeper, Tacama sighed once more and said, "You're not making this very easy, are you?" Astrid straightened, finally finding enough courage to speak out.

"You shouldn't be surprised," she remarked. "We haven't exactly had the most pleasant time here in Tolico."

"You can say that again…" Hitomi muttered under her breath.

Tacama nodded and took another step forward, this

time reaching for something at his waist before placing it on the floor. The metal object glimmered in the blue light, revealing it to be a dagger quite similar to the one in Moha's possession.

"I've heard of your ordeal, both of you. I can only offer my most sincere apologies my ladies. Please trust me when I say that I mean no harm to either of you. I surrender my only weapon and I trust that you will take this as my word." Tacama stated, his voice remaining soft and solemn. "You were brought to Tolico because of the color of your eyes, isn't that right?" He soon continued speaking before they were able to respond, "I am sure the two of you are extremely confused at discovering that you aren't the only ones with blue eyes. I don't wish to confuse you more but alas…"

With the snap of his fingers, candles began to light on the walls, the room becoming filled with firelight. The room looked like it was filled with sunlight, making them forget that they were inside an ancient pyramid. With the light blaring through the room, Astrid no longer had to squint to see clearly. Now both of them were able to see Tacama clearly in the light.

Instantly, Astrid noticed that Tacama was unlike the people of Tolico. He had burnt umber hair which looked illuminated within the firelight, almost as if his hair was a gentle flame. His skin was slightly paler than most of the people in Tolico, but not nearly as pale as Hitomi. His attire was similar to how the people dressed within the palace; wearing a knee length kilt with a large belt adorned with dozens of sapphire and emerald gems.

However, the most peculiar thing about Tacama was not his odd hair or the lightness of his skin, but the color of his eyes. Even though Astrid wasn't close enough to see clearly, she knew for sure that she had seen a shimmer of blue within his irises. As he stepped closer towards them,

Astrid's suspicion was now confirmed, both of them now being able to see his blue eyes flickering in the light.

He smiled at their shocked expressions and continued, "Blue eyes are not as rare as you think, or perhaps our world is incredibly small." Tacama grinned and ruffled his hand through his hair. "Now, let us go and settle this confusion, shall we?" He turned away from the girls and began walking down a hallway to the right.

Hitomi and Astrid exchanged a look of both fear and curiosity. Before Astrid could say anything, Hitomi jutted forward, grabbing the dagger and they both began to follow him down the hallway. The girls followed Tacama a few feet behind; Hitomi keeping a wary eye out for Tacama whilst arming herself with his dagger.

After a few minutes, Astrid nudged Hitomi's shoulder and said in a whisper, "Stop doing that. He's obviously not going to kill us. And how is he supposed to harm us when you have his dagger?"

But Hitomi remained steadfast in her suspicion, telling Astrid about all the possible ways that he could kill them both.

"You don't have to stop her Astrid. She's only protecting herself and I knew she'd take my dagger." Tacama said in a calm tone. He paused and turned towards Astrid and Hitomi, calmly stating, "Anyone would try to protect themselves, it's perfectly normal. I can assure you though that I won't harm either of you, I am only here to help you." He looked to his right and nodded towards them both. "Now if you can come this way." He said before walking into a room that appeared unnoticeable from where Astrid stood.

The room wasn't considerably large, it was sculpted from limestone and was lit with dozens of small torches hanging from the walls. The lighting wasn't nearly as breathtaking as that they had seen in the hall, but it made up for it through the beautifully painted maroon walls that possessed intricate Aztec carvings.

"The blue 'stars' you saw were keys, similar to the pendants you wear around your necks. Those pendants are the key to unlocking the many gates to the Lake. Many years ago, those pendants were given to people with special blue eyes, people like us." Tacama said, strolling across the room to a group of four chairs and made a gesture to the girls to sit down.

Hitomi and Astrid exchanged glances, still unsure about Tacama's intentions.

"I can assure you, if I had planned on killing either one of you I would have already done it." Tacama sighed, sitting down in the center chair that mimicked the centering and appearance of a throne. "Now, please sit. I know you two have been walking for a while, I'm sure your legs would appreciate it if you sat down and you should have something to drink." Tacama said gently, his voice reassuring them both that he is here to help. Hitomi nodded slowly and gave a slight shove at Astrid.

The girls sat down across from each other and stared at Tacama, Hitomi displaying an annoyed glare as if to say *Talk, but make it quick.*

"Do either one of you know why you are in Tolico?" Tacama asked.

"Moha has a strong craving for people with blue eyes and it just so happens that Astrid and I have them." Hitomi growled.

"Sort of... You see, I knew Moha personally"

"How personal?" Astrid demanded, her chest suddenly feeling numb and her trust in Tacama began to dwindle. Tacama looked extremely uncomfortable, realizing that what he was about to say would be met with anger.

Despite that, he still continued, "I know you were in contact with my mother, Xoco, I'm surprised she never told you." He then muttered, "Moha is my brother."

Astrid stood up immediately, knocking her chair over from the shock. Her whole body began to feel weak and numb. She attempted to compose herself in asking Tacama, "Are you trying to say that Moha's servant is his *and* your mother? You're all family?"

"Well… yes. Moha wasn't always the person you know him as now. He was once very kind hearted, as well as being a little strange but he was always very kind." Tacama implored for them to listen as he shifted a little. "Let me explain. Thirteen years ago, my brother took the throne of Tolico. By took I mean stole. He had brutally murdered my father, the rightful king of Tolico. He killed my younger sister and imprisoned my mother." Both of them could tell that this was hard for Tacama to say.

He stood up from his chair and continued, "Moha had also killed my wife and my newborn son. This pyramid is very special as it possesses a great power. It is connected to thousands of pathways which are interlinked through the lake. Access to the lake allows you to cross through different realms and dimensions that we cannot even imagine! In order to protect the pyramid's power, I faked my death and stayed here in the Tolico pyramid. If Moha ever gains control over this pyramid, he will cross through into different realms and will kill millions. Somehow, Moha has managed to find a gateway into the lake that was previously undiscovered. That is how he managed to get the two of you to Tolico so quickly."

"Can you take us home?" Hitomi asked eagerly. "I mean, if you can basically travel anywhere, you can take us home then, right?"

Tacama nodded, "Well yes, of course."

Astrid paused. She couldn't understand why she was feeling unsure of herself. She had just found out that there is a way to go back to Egypt. She had a chance to go home.

However, her chest felt heavy, as if it was being strapped down by a ton of bricks.

"We could go home, but Moha would still have access to this secret gate. We wouldn't be helping anyone but ourselves…" she muttered, looking at Hitomi for a while and then over at Tacama. "You'd still be left here and Moha would still bring more people to be sacrificed."

Tacama sighed, "Well yes but…"

"Then I want to stay!" Astrid commanded. Hitomi jumped out of her chair instantly.

"Stay? You've been preaching about how much you want to go home! Now you have a way back to Egypt and you want to stay? You could be killed!"

"Yes!" Astrid yelled at Hitomi. "I'd die if it meant this kingdom was safe. I don't care if I never see Egypt again. If I went home, I would be filled with guilt, knowing that thousands more just like you and I would be dying on this forsaken island!" Astrid looked at Tacama, who seemed taken aback by it all.

"I want to stay," she repeated, "I want to help you. Take Hitomi home if she wants but I can't leave yet. Xoco had said that there were hundreds of people Moha has killed and if we don't do something about it, then hundreds more will be killed. I don't want anyone else to experience what we have been through. Never again!"

Tacama froze and was surprised by Astrid's courage. But was he really going to let a fifteen-year-old girl strike a rebellion against his brother? Most of all, was he going to let her die here when he could save her by sending her home?

"Answer me gatekeeper." Astrid demanded.

This island needs to be restored to it's former glory. I have no right to stop her from helping. But would it be wise to let this girl stay behind and fight? Tacama thought for a while, considering what options he had left in restoring

Tolico. Finally, he came to a decision.

"Fine." Tacama said. "You may stay." He then dropped down into a bow. "I pledge my allegiance to you my lady, I shall be your ally in the rebellion against King Moha, until death strikes me down."

Astrid knelt in front of him like a royal guard. "To the death." She agreed.

Hitomi, who had remained silent since her outburst suddenly knelt in front of Astrid and whispered, "To the death."

Even though these three came from different kingdoms and abided by different cultures, they all knew that a pledge of allegiance towards each other held the utmost importance. The three of them knew that they were now bound by their vow to save Tolico, even if it's to the death.

Until Death Strikes us Down

Thirteen years ago...

Prince Tacama was an exceptionally tall and slender man, which was an unusual trait for men of Tolico. He was the middle child, with his eldest brother Moha who was six years older and his youngest sister Izel, who was just ten years old. Tacama was seen as a frail child due to his thin physique and he was favored less by his parents due to his frailty. But Tacama felt that he possessed something very special, something that neither Moha or Izel had.

He had a family of his own. Two years ago, Tacama's father had rescued a beautiful young woman named Alana from an unknown kingdom she called Azori. Much like Tacama, Alana had stunning blue eyes that resembled the deepest ocean. A year after their meeting, Tacama and Alana had married. Soon after their marriage, Alana had become pregnant. They were blessed with a son. Tacama felt such joy, he considered himself to be the luckiest man alive. However, days after their son's birth, things took a turn for the worse.

Tacama was always proud of his father. Necalli was known as a hero in Tolico, for traveling to distant lands to fight for people who couldn't fight for themselves. Some had even treated the king as though he were a god amongst the people. Even though the man was nearing the age of sixty, he still felt as strong as when he was sixteen. However one day, as Tacama entered his father's throne room, he didn't appear as strong as he should have. Necalli was hunched over in his throne, a worried expression carved into his face.

"Father?" Tacama asked, "Is everything alright?" Necalli looked up and smiled, as if a grin could conceal the turmoil brewing within him.

"Oh yes! Yes, everything is alright my boy." He said, standing from his throne. "Tacama, could you do a favor for me?" Tacama nodded. "Good, good! I need you to go to the pyramid for me. I just need you to check on everything for me, make sure that you lock up all the gates." Necalli smiled reassuringly once more. Tacama didn't think he had seen his father smile so often in his entire life. Even though the grin was meant to make Tacama feel better, he couldn't help but feel doubt weighing down his chest.

"Of course father." He muttered.

In noticing Tacama's uncertainty, Necalli yelled out to him. "Nothing to worry about!" He gasped before lowering his voice into a quieter tone. "You see, it's a robber. He's getting a little too close to the nobles it seems, getting too cocky. Just to be safe, go to the pyramid. I'm sure this man won't do anything stupid but we just want to keep everyone safe. I'm sure you understand."

"Oh, alright." Tacama breathed a sigh in relief. His father nodded and of course another smile.

"That's all. I'll make sure to watch after Alana and the baby and to tell them where you're going. Just come back in the morning and tell me how everything goes." Tacama did as he was told and went to the Tolico pyramid on horseback. The pyramid might have looked small but the inside appeared larger than the Tolican palace.

Perhaps the pyramid worked as a palace at one time. Tacama thought to himself. It was certainly large enough and it even had a beautiful throne room. Perhaps it was childish, but Tacama had liked this room the most. After he had locked all the gates to the lake, Tacama had decided to take a break in the throne room. Although three of the dozens of bed chambers within the pyramid were completely furnished, Tacama chose to rest in the throne room. It was always far more comfortable than the one he had, though he wasn't exactly sure why. The throne was made from wood with a strip of leather down the middle to work as a poor excuse for a cushion. However, something about it was still comfortable to Tacama and it felt like it belonged to him. As if it was meant for him.

He leaned his head against the hard backing of the chair and let his eyes rest, hoping he could find some comfort in this peaceful refuge. He had never liked the silence that the pyramid possessed. Perhaps it was because Tacama was raised in the loud bustle of the palace.

Gods, what would it be like to have to deal with this silence all the time, he thought. Suddenly, the sound of the warning bells rang through the pyramid from the center of Tolico. Something had happened in the palace. *That robber wouldn't be so bold*, Tacama thought, rushing out of the throne room and down the hall to the entrance. His mind filled with panic. *What could be happening?*

Tacama ran out of the pyramid and threw himself onto his horse before taking off across the river. The midnight air was filled with the scent of blood. *What's happening?* Tacama thought to himself. Once Tacama reached the palace, the royal guards had rushed passed him, nearly shoving him off of his horse.

"What's happening?" He yelled as he pushed his horse through the crowd. It was as if no one could hear him. He eyed a guard charging beside him and Tacama reached for the hair of the man, wrenching it tightly and pulling his face towards him, grabbing his full attention.

"I *demand* an answer! I am the prince of Tolico! *What is happening?*" He yelled into the guards face.

"The king has been attacked!" The guard choked out,

a look of terror shot through his eyes. Tacama's heart dropped. He released the guard and continued to push his horse forward.

"Let me through!" He bellowed at the men below him, but very few obliged. At last he reached the palace doors, Tacama climbed down from his horse and abruptly slammed himself into the door, making sure that he got through on the first ram. There were very few people who appeared to be inside. *Were all of the guards just waiting outside? What were they doing?* Tacama unsheathed his sword and charged down the main hall and down to the throne room.

"Father!" Tacama called out. "Father, where are you?" He turned the corner and was faced with a closed door. He kicked at it until it broke loose and pushed it open with brute force.

His father was no longer on his throne. He was on the floor, lying on his stomach, his dark eyes blank and lost. His clothes had been torn and smears of blood stained his robes. Blood pooled around his balding head. Tacama noticed that his fathers crown was missing. *Has someone done this for his crown?* Tacama couldn't feel his legs, they were slowly giving way, causing him to stumble as he attempted to move forward. His fingers were beginning to loosen around his sword. He wasn't able to comprehend what he saw in front of him.

His father was dead. Despite the loss he felt, at wanting to rush over to his father, he realized that he had no time to waste. Soon his mind began to race, wondering where the rest of his family were. *Where is mother? Moha, Izel, Alana?* Tacama knew his father could not be saved and so, with a heavy heart, he turned away from Necalli's corpse and went down the hall to the royal bed-chambers.

He called out for his sister as he came near her room. No response. Tacama was left with a sharp pain in his stomach. Her door was open but she wasn't in her bed.

"Izel?" He whispered, feeling like the breath had been taken from his lungs. He walked around the bed but couldn't find her there either. Suddenly, he felt something against his foot and he looked down to find the object. Instead of an object, he found a bloodied hand. It was Izel's limp hand, which lay just beside Tacama's sandal. He squeezed his eyes shut, tears beginning to streak his face. He was afraid of what he would find beneath the bed, but he knew that he needed to look. Going down onto his knees, he lowered his head and slowly, he opened his eyes and turned his head to look. He felt sick at what he found.

Izel was on her side, still holding on tightly to a doll their mother had made for her. There was a single slit across her throat, blood covering her neck like a ruby choker. He noticed that her happy blue eyes were nothing but bloodied holes. There was no use in checking for a heartbeat. He couldn't just leave his sister there. He slowly pulled her limp body out from underneath and laid her down on her bed, tucking her in as if Izel was going to sleep. Tacama picked up his sword and stood once more, numbly walking towards Izel's door, the pain in his stomach beginning to worsen.

Once again, he called out the names of his family, hoping for a response. But no one replied. He began to scream for his family, yelling at the top of his lungs hoping that someone would hear him. Tacama felt as though that was the only thing he could do and so he continued.

"Mother! Alana!" He yelled until his throat felt like it was being ripped apart. He had finally arrived at his mother's bedchamber, he swung open the door. No one was inside, the bed was empty, she was nowhere to be found. Xoco was gone. Hope filled Tacama, thinking that maybe his mother was still alive. He *had* to find her. He went back to the main hall and called out again, even though his throat hurt when he spoke.

At last, a voice finally replied back to Tacama. At first, Tacama could barely hear it but it soon became clearer.

"Tacama!" Alana yelled. *She's alive!* Tacama thought. Clearing his throat, Tacama attempted to yell out to his wife, but it still hurt.

"I'm coming!" He called back, rushing to the sound of his wife's voice. He came near their bedchamber and opened the door, a grin stretching from cheek to cheek. However, as soon as he saw his room, his smile stopped. Alana was lying on the floor, life slowly leaving her body. Just like Izel, Alana's eyes were nothing but bloodied holes. A deep wound lay in her stomach, blood was slowly seeping out. She whispered Tacama's name, getting weaker by the second.

"I'm here." Tacama said quietly, falling to his knees beside her. "I'm here, Alana." He touched her cheek gently and brushed back her hair.

"Tacama… It hurts." She choked, her breathing become slower. Amidst her blood spluttered chokes, she could barely be heard, "I'm so sorry." Her teeth chattered in pain and her weak arm went from the wound in her stomach to Tacama's hand at her cheek. "He took him! He took our son!"

"Who? Who took him?" Tacama asked, trying his hardest not to show any pain in his voice. Alana's shaking slowed.

"Moha," she breathed heavily. "Moha, he went mad! He went after everyone and he took our son."

"He wouldn't do anything," Tacama paused and chose not to question her. He knew Alana's time was short and she knew it too. Tacama pulled his wife into his arms and let out a heavy sigh.

Seeing his wife slowly dying made his body tremble with fear, but he needed to remain strong for her. He whispered to Alana, "I'll find our son, I promise. Don't worry Alana, it's going to be alright." Tacama brushed back her hair and whispered to her soothingly, "Remember what I said when we first met? You were hurt, your leg was broken and you thought you were going to die."

Despite the pain, Alana managed to smile and said, "I overreacted."

Tacama nodded, crying but laughing at the same time. "I knew that but I didn't care. I knew you were scared so I told you I'd stay by your side." Alana chuckled but it came out more like a groan.

"'Until death strikes us down.' That's what you said."

"Exactly." Tacama whispered and leaned forward, placing a kiss on Alana's forehead.

Her shaking stopped entirely and an overwhelming numbness replaced the hope that once filled Tacama's heart. Just like his sister, Tacama laid Alana on their bed and placed the cover over her chest before leaving the room.

This time, he didn't yell, there was nothing left inside of him. Tacama's name was echoing through the hall, but this time it was in a mocking tone. Tacama ran down the corridor and into the sparring room where he heard laughing.

Moha was standing in the middle of the room, bent over and laughing with his sword in his hand.

"Oh Tacama, save me, save me!" He sputtered. He then stopped laughing, doing nothing for a moment and then, he pointed his sword at Tacama.

"You look as though all hope has left you." He slowly cocked his head to the side, a grin emerging along his lips and his dark eyes were displaying a type of sadistic joy.

"Poor thing. Father's dead. Izel's dead. Your wife is dead. Your son is dead and you will soon be dead as well. Oh, what pain must be festering within you little brother." He smiled hysterically at Tacama, baring his teeth like a wolf.

"What are you doing?" Tacama muttered in shock, still unable to believe what he is seeing.

"What am I doing?" Moha laughed. "What am *I* doing? I'm living out my destiny! Father is dead now! I am king!" He threw his head back and began laughing maniacally. "Long live the king!" He cried out. "Long live me!"

Tacama didn't know what to do. The thought of stopping him seemed impossible.

"You're insane!" Tacama choked out. "You're absolutely insane."

Moha rubbed his fist against his stubble and said hoarsely, "I'm insane? That's a little harsh don't you think?"

"You killed our family!"

"Our *family?*" A look of confusion was etched across Moha's face. He suddenly said, "Oh yes. Them... That was all necessary you see. Let me explain. Father knew this all along, he knew my fate was *this*. He did this all for me Tacama, all of it. Taking in Alana? He only did that because of her eyes. They host something god-like in them and the only way you can get to it is by killing them and feasting on their pretty blue eyes." He began laughing once more, yelling out, "I'm a god Tacama! I'm a real god!"

Tacama was paralyzed with fear. *What had Moha done? Did he eat Izel's eyes? Alana's as well? What did he think he was doing?*

Moha gave Tacama a sly grin, whispering, "You look like you're about to kill me. But there's terror in those eyes, you can't kill me. I'm your brother, so run. I'll let you, I'll let you run and hide for as long as you want. It's late, go to sleep and come back when the sun rises. Come back when you're ready Tacama."

Tacama knew better, he couldn't fight his brother. Moha was bigger, stronger, and he has more willpower than Tacama does. Tacama tried to think like his father, what was the best thing to do? Fight and possibly die? No... no,

Tacama didn't want to die. He didn't want to fall along with the bodies of his family. He had to protect the last thing he possibly could, the pyramid. That pyramid could go to different realms, just like the one that Alana came from. Tacama knew that if Moha got access to the pyramid, he could find other people with blue eyes and kill them too and Tacama couldn't let that happen. He may have not been able to save his family, but maybe he could save someone else's.

. He turned away from his brother and walked out of the door like a scared dog with his tail between his legs. He pushed his way through the royal guards who were now panicking and scrambling everywhere like headless chickens. He climbed up onto his horse and rode back to the pyramid. He buried the stone deep within the dirt, hiding the lock of the pyramid from sight. As fatigue and deep sadness took hold he dragged himself through the building and sat down in his throne.

"If there is one thing I can do, it is to protect the people of the realms," he whispered to himself the words of his father. His voice bounced off the walls but the silence engulfed him seconds later. Sitting in the silence, he thought that perhaps this throne was meant to be his and he was meant to be the protector. He was meant to rule the silence and he did for thirteen years. All those long years he waited for the sun to rise and for the night to finally end.

The Rebellion Begins

As Astrid, Hitomi and Tacama sat down, they realized that they needed to think about their plan of action.

With the silence creeping in, Astrid asked Tacama, "So what do we do first? How do we stop Moha?"

Stroking his chin with the tips of his fingers, thinking about the best possible option, Tacama finally said, "First, we have to lock the gate to which Moha has access. Unfortunately, I have no idea where it is. So the next best thing to do is to steal the key." Tacama sighed in realizing the difficulty of their task.

"How do we do that?" Hitomi asked with a hint of doubt in her voice whilst she crossed her arms. Tacama bit down on his bottom lip, a look of worry etched into his face.

"We have no other option but to go after him. It is vital that we get that key. Without it, Moha will be unable to capture and kill innocent people with blue eyes. For many years now I have tried to find the secret gate. It is hidden too well for anyone to locate. It is pointless to continue searching for it, so our priority is the key…"

Hitomi's jaw dropped as soon as she heard his proposal of confronting Moha. "Go after him? That's crazy! We don't stand a chance against that beast." She yelled.

Astrid tried to remain calm at the thought of going against Moha. Adding to Hitomi's argument, she asked Tacama in a nervous voice, "So, if we are to successfully get the key, we would need to kill him, wouldn't we?"

Despite Astrid's courage in wanting to defend the people of the realms and her hatred towards Moha, the thought of killing a human being shook her body to the core.

With a look of regret, Tacama nodded and said, "That man is no longer my brother. In order to protect the people, we will have to kill him."

Upon hearing this, Astrid cleared her throat and said, "Well, I suppose it isn't going to be a simple task. We all know how strong he is and it would be hard for any of us to ever overpower him. I agree with Hitomi to some extent, the three of us together are no match against Moha. But, we could try to catch him off guard, giving us an advantage. But before we plan our assault on Moha, we need to know what the key looks like. Does he have it with him at all times? Perhaps he keeps it within his bedchamber. I have been in there once and I noticed that his golden chest contains a number of treasures. Maybe the key is kept within the chest?"

Tacama shook his head and said, "No. He wouldn't leave the key exposed. Fortunately, I know what the key is. Mother has told me that the obsidian dagger that he carries is the key. The good thing is that as boys, we were taught how to throw knives; he's always been a fan of it. I'm certain we can enrage him, just enough in making him throw his blade… We just need to make sure that we don't get hit by it."

Feeling disappointed at Tacama's plan, Hitomi slammed the palm of her hand against her knee in a fit of rage and cried out, "That's your plan? We will surely be killed the moment he sees us. This is madness. We don't even have any weapons!"

"We have your sword, Hitomi," said Astrid in a slightly calmer tone, hoping that Hitomi would soon quiet down.

Tacama stood from his chair and unsheathed his sword, calmly stating to Hitomi, "I have my sword as well."

Hitomi furrowed her thin brows, still feeling dubious about their plan. "We have three people and only two blades. Not exactly the most fearsome group. And Astrid will need a weapon; she will need to defend herself when the time comes."

Tacama turned away from the girls and went to the back wall. A torch was suddenly lit above him, illuminating a small golden chest in front of him. It glistened beautifully in the firelight, shining like the sun. It was as if he had made this chest emerge from the darkness. His voice echoed gently when he stated to them both, "I have a solution to that." He opened the chest and said, "I believe that when a sword is in someone's possession, it should stay there until their owner dies. So Hitomi, your sword is yours alone, as is mine. As for you Astrid..." Tacama rose from the golden chest with a small object in his hand and turned back to Astrid.

"This had belonged to my father, it was a gift from my wife. As my father is no longer with us, I believe that his weapon requires a new owner. Alana felt it appropriate to give my father this weapon as he was renowned for being the great soldier who traveled to different kingdoms, fighting for the weak and vulnerable. He had a great passion for helping others. It seems Astrid, that you are much like my father. A great warrior who will stop at nothing in order to protect the people. Alana called this blade an Azuli sword, a sword of the Azera – a secret society for people just like my father and yourself. A society for heroes."

Tacama presented the object to Astrid, revealing a golden triangle as big as his hand. Astrid noticed that the symbol on the triangle was identical to the one she had seen on the center of the lapis pyramid. Tacama pressed the center of the symbol with his thumb, revealing itself to being a locking mechanism. Suddenly, a long lapis blade emerged from the base of the triangle. It was unlike any other weapon that Astrid had seen. It was slightly larger than a dagger and yet it was smaller than a sword. The blade itself had a beautifully intricate pattern along its center, the flames highlighted the golden swirls of the pattern, making them glisten like starlight.

Both Astrid and Hitomi were mesmerized by the beauty of the lapis blade, reflecting the dance of the flames within its glowing form. However, Astrid noticed something along the edge of the blade, it was barely visible within the firelight. It was a small etching of a phrase in an unknown language. Astrid became curious about the foreign phrase, wondering what the message was. Tacama turned his hand over to reveal two leather straps which were wrapped over his hand securely. The straps were connected to the triangular object, making it easier to hold and maneuver. This was definitely a unique weapon for Astrid to observe.

"This is an Azuli sword," Tacama said, a smile beginning to form along his face. "It is unlike any other weapon ever created by a mortal man. I believe my father would be happy to know that you are now the owner of the Azuli sword." He pressed the symbol again, forcing the blade to retreat within the triangle. He then slid the straps from his hand and held the golden triangle before Astrid, waiting for her to accept the gift.

She took it from him, softly whispering her thanks to Tacama. She pulled the straps tight over her own palm before activating the Azuli sword once more. There was something about it that felt natural to Astrid as she firmly gripped the hilt of the weapon.

"This blade was meant for a hero." Tacama said. "Can you become the hero that Tolico needs?"

Astrid shook her head, looking up at Tacama and said, "Perhaps not alone, but with both of you helping me I think I can."

Hitomi smiled and nodded, saying in an eager tone "OK, I think we can manage that."

"It's been a long and strange day, so I feel it's time that you returned to your previous location. I will speak with mother and explain what has happened. There is no point on delay, we will strike the enemy quickly, our assault will take place tomorrow. Until then, rest. I imagine that the days ahead of us will be filled with many difficulties."

Tacama began to lead both Astrid and Hitomi out of the pyramid. Neither of them spoke a word, their plan of attack finally sinking into their minds.

Tacama broke the silence in saying, "Tonight, I shall escort you both back to Xoco and tomorrow I will come for you." Hitomi and Astrid nodded in acknowledgment. Whilst they were following Tacama, Astrid couldn't help but notice Hitomi's unnatural silence. She began to wonder if Hitomi was having second thoughts about their plan. Was she thinking that they had made a bad decision? Was this rebellion going too fast? Astrid felt confident in their plan and knew that she could trust Tacama, but it looked as if Hitomi was holding back.

Astrid walked slower in an attempt to get Hitomi's attention. She knew Tacama would probably hear whatever she was going to say, but she knew that he wouldn't eavesdrop in on their conversation. And she felt that it would be better if she and Hitomi had some sort of privacy, even if privacy meant a few yards away from Tacama. Hitomi noticed Astrid's slow pace and soon got the message. She too slowed her pace, annoyed that Astrid realized something was wrong.

"What?" She growled under her breath.

"You seem a little… off. I just wanted to know if everything is alright. Is it?" Astrid whispered, giving a concerned glance at Hitomi, hoping that she would open up.

After a moment of silence, Hitomi said, "The last time I saw Moha, I was nothing but a coward. I was afraid, a frightened little girl who wanted to run away. I don't want to be that little girl again. I don't want to be afraid to fight! But all I feel right now is fear." Hitomi looked over at Astrid, a look of doubt and fear hidden behind her furrowed brows, but Astrid knew better. Even though the two of them had only been together for a short time and Astrid is no professional at knowing Hitomi's personal traits, but she knew that Hitomi was in a dark place. She needed some reassurance from a friend.

As Astrid opened her mouth to speak, another voice interjected immediately.

"I understand that your time in Tolico has been dreadful, being stuck in a foreign realm and feeling cut off from everything you know. But I do understand the fear that you felt when you faced Moha. That type of fear doesn't fade away, it only festers inside you and turns into something... awful." Tacama said, stopping in his tracks.

His voice was strong and confident, showing no fear at all. He turned towards the girls and crossed his arms. He said to them, "Both of you may be terrified now and you have every reason to be frightened. But you can't let your fears consume you. You are both brave and determined, that much is clear. Anyone can see that you girls are dedicated to helping others and will stop at nothing. You had the strength to run away from Moha and to live on your own within this foreign land. You are strong enough to face him again, both of you. Neither of you are cowards. I had the chance to end Moha's madness many years ago, but I didn't, I just couldn't. I am ashamed of myself for being unable to end his barbarity. So I shall say this to you both, do not be afraid; all of this has happened for a reason. It is the will of the gods that we will not die here, I promise you that."

The sun was beginning to fall behind the horizon by the time Hitomi and Astrid had gone back to their shack. As

Tacama bid them farewell, Astrid and Hitomi had remained silent. Hitomi sat on her cot and Astrid sat on the floor, not ready to go to sleep just yet. The only communication between the two was through their exchange of glances. Neither of them could conjure up a sentence. It was as if they had run out of words to use.

The silence was overwhelming; Astrid could barely deal with it anymore. She then cried out, "Why won't you talk Hitomi! Have I said something or done something? Say something!"

Hitomi mumbled into her cup, her voice low which made it sound like a hum. Astrid was getting annoyed and confused at why she didn't want to talk. She continued to pester Hitomi with the same question, waiting for her to break.

Hitomi cursed under her breath, slamming her cup onto the floor and yelled at Astrid, "I envy you!"

"Envy me?!" Astrid gasped in shock.

"*Yes!*" Hitomi yelled, pounding her fists into the floor.

"Yes, I envy you! You've been here for, what, a week? And now, you get to go home! I've been here for years Astrid, years! I don't even have a home to go back to. And now I'm being pushed into some kind of rebellion. I couldn't fight Moha then and I know I can't fight him now. I tried to act brave back in the pyramid but in reality, I am scared Astrid. You're being naive; you're trusting some man you just met and you're vowing an allegiance to him? No wonder you got kidnapped! You trust people you've just met and you assume everyone is trustworthy. You're being so stupid!"

Anger was starting to build up within Astrid. Her chest began feeling heavy, she clenched her fingers together, digging deeper and deeper into her skin. She stood up immediately, feeling too enraged to quietly remain seated. She was angry and confused at Hitomi, why did Hitomi feel this way? *I was only trying to help!* Astrid couldn't stay quiet a moment longer.

"I'm the stupid one?" She barked out and suddenly, all of her frustration poured out like a waterfall. "I'm stupid for trying to get out of this situation? For trusting someone who has sworn to help us? Why is it wrong that I want to do something? At least I'm not being a coward and hiding in this *forsaken shack* for the rest of my life because I'm too afraid to face my fears! I wasn't kidnapped by Moha because I trusted him, believe me. I wanted him out of my country, I told him that. He had some assassin kidnap me in my sleep and drug me. I couldn't do anything about it, just like you couldn't do anything to prevent your kidnapping. You don't need to feel like you're weak. You don't have to let your fears overwhelm you. I am just as frightened as you are. I'm sorry you don't have a family to return to, but that doesn't mean you should stay here while Moha is wreaking havoc across all the realms!"

"Where else would I go? Back to your kingdom?" Hitomi scoffed, crossing her arms over her chest. Pausing for a moment, Astrid realized that it wasn't a bad idea, Hitomi could come with her.

"Exactly!" Astrid said with an exasperated sigh and she finally sat down. Looking annoyed and tired from yelling, Astrid said in a low tone, "You may be a brat half the time, but you still took me in and you didn't have to do that. You could have left me to die but you took me into your home. What kind of person would I be if I didn't pay you back? You don't deserve to live in this prison forever, away from the rest of the world. I know you can't go back to Japan, that no one would welcome you into the kingdom or believe that you are their princess. The least I can do is take you back to mine. My family is still alive, they're still looking for me and they'll know immediately that you are my friend. You don't have to separate yourself from everyone. You helped me, can't you for once let someone help you?"

Silence hung in the air. Hitomi was surprised at hearing that she would be welcomed into a home. Her lips trembled and tears welled up in her eyes. But doubt still lingered in her mind.

She looked down, preventing Astrid from seeing her in this state. She then mumbled, "You wouldn't do that. No one would take in a stranger."

Astrid shook her head and grinned at Hitomi's stubborn nature, saying, "Yes I would, you deserve it. You deserve a home of your own, a family of your own."

The Sun Rises

As the first rays of the sun lit up the darkness of the forest, Astrid was awoken by the sound of someone knocking on the wooden door.

"Hitomi? Astrid? Are you in there?" Called Xoco from outside. Astrid looked over sleepily at Hitomi, who was already awake. Hitomi pulled her cover away and walked to the door. It took a while for Astrid to realize that she had fallen asleep on the floor, being mentally exhausted from their argument last night, she literally dropped where she stood. Well, at least she had the soft grass mat beneath her. As Hitomi opened the door, she was met by Xoco who came eagerly rushing in with three large wicker baskets that were filled with fruits. Both of them noticed that Xoco was in high spirits this morning as she had a smile beaming across her face. Just as Hitomi went to close the door, Tacama came in with baskets as well.

"I knew you'd be hungry." Xoco said, setting her baskets down beside the fireplace.

Tacama rolled his eyes, smiling at his mother's generosity and said, "As I told you before mother, I don't think the entire kingdom of Tolico could be hungry enough to eat all of this fruit." He laughed heartily. Astrid noticed a change in Tacama's behavior, how different he seemed to be around his mother.

It was at that moment that Astrid noticed the connection between the two of them. She couldn't help but smile at how happy Tacama behaved when he was near Xoco, not having to worry about the realms or Moha. Those worries were so far away for Tacama. Their bond reminded Astrid about her connection with her own parents, how close they were and how she longed to be with them.

"This is definitely more than enough Xoco." Hitomi said whilst grabbing a papaya from one of the baskets and returning to her cot. "It should last us a few days, I'm sure."

She grabbed a knife from beside her and sliced the fruit in two, the juices flowing down her hand. She waved one half of the papaya toward Astrid, waiting for her to take the juicy fruit which Astrid gratefully did and began to devour it.

"Do we have any sort of plan?" Hitomi asked Xoco, ignoring Tacama entirely. Xoco did not reply, but the question was answered by another.

"Somewhat." Tacama said, taking a bite out of a crispy apple. With his mouth partially full, he continued to say, "I have been thinking that it would be better if mother and I did the actual fighting and you two will be used as bait."

Midway in biting the papaya, Astrid coughed abruptly and spluttered to Tacama, "Bait?"

Seeing the surprise in Astrid's eyes, Tacama sighed and began to elaborate. "Yes, bait. Let me explain. Both of you will be fighting - in a way. You will both be used as decoys to some extent, one will be fighting Moha, keeping him occupied whilst the other will retrieve the dagger. I understand the difficulty of this task but it is the most plausible plan. And both of you need to make sure that he does not spot either myself or mother, things will only get worse if he sees us. As I said yesterday, Moha's main defense is throwing blades. I'm quite certain that as soon as he sees you two, he will be too enraged to think logically and will throw his dagger in response. Now, the one retrieving the blade must have very quick reflexes. We can't afford any mistakes. A slightest falter will result in our downfall for sure."

Astrid and Hitomi looked at each other, wondering if this plan was too much for two girls to deploy successfully. Their eyes were full of fear as they realized the pressure that now rested on their shoulders. Instantly, Hitomi looked up and swallowed a piece of fruit. Hiding the doubt in her eyes, she said, "I can fight, I've been hunting for years. There can't be much of a difference between hunting and attacking. I'm sure I can get his attention away from you, even if it's only for a moment."

Tacama nodded and said with relief, "Good. I'm sure you will do well." He turned to Astrid and asked her, "Astrid, do you think you can retrieve the dagger? Remember, you're going to have to be a target. He will go after you so you'll need to grab the dagger and get out of there as fast as you can."

Astrid thought a moment, wondering if she was capable of doing something as courageous as this. Their whole plan rested on her ability to get the dagger swiftly. *Could I really do that?*

"Astrid can do it." Hitomi interjected as she walked over to Astrid and threw her arm around her shoulder. "She's good at getting herself into trouble. I know Moha isn't going to be pleased in seeing his newest princess coming back to fight him. She can handle it." Hitomi proudly declared to Tacama, her smile emitting such pride in Astrid that you wouldn't think fear was lingering in her mind.

But Astrid was taken aback by the amount of trust they have in her. She began to doubt herself, her eyes downcast.

"Should you really be putting so much trust in me...?" Astrid mumbled.

This time Xoco spoke. "Well of course." She said and a kind, motherly smile emerged, making Astrid feel at ease. "You were brave enough to escape from Moha. So I know that you'll be brave enough to do this."

Tacama grinned and said, "You will be magnificent."

Astrid was finding it hard to believe that these people had so much faith in her. They were willing to place the freedom of Tolico on her shoulders. If they believed that she could do this, then perhaps she needed to have more faith in herself.

Looking up at the three of them, she finally said, "Alright, I'll do it

As the four of them prepared to leave the forest, the reality of their plan began to sink into Astrid's mind. There was no turning back now. Xoco led them through a secret route that went through the darkest parts of the woodland and finally ended at the house in which Astrid and Hitomi had been held captive. It made sense how Xoco managed to continually come to them and return to the palace without being seen. Seeing the house again brought back many memories for the girls. To come back willingly felt extremely strange for them both. Astrid could only imagine how Tacama felt, coming back to his home after so many years and to witness the madness of Moha once again. As Xoco ushered them towards the house, she made them wait outside.

"All of you stay here until I call you." Xoco said, giving a heavy sigh as she looked to the back door of the house. Hitomi crossed her arms over her chest and furrowed her brows.

"Wait here?" She scoffed, "You can't really expect us to wait out here. We might get caught by the soldiers. And what are we supposed to wait for? Some kind of sign? Are we supposed to stand here until the god of fire comes to invite us inside?" Hitomi was in no mood for games, she wanted to get this over and done with.

Tacama grinned ever so slightly in an attempt to keep from laughing. The tenacity of Hitomi amused him. But he composed himself and sternly said, "Lower your tone

Hitomi. Mother has a point. If we go charging in blindly, we will surely get caught. At least she will be able check if it is clear for us to continue. We will wait here, it is safer." And so they waited for Xoco to return.

Shortly after Xoco entered the house, Astrid caught sight of a group of barrels and boxes that lay near the back door. She made a gesture to both Tacama and Hitomi, indicating that they should hide there until Xoco returned. Nodding in agreement, the three of them went swiftly to the pile, keeping a careful eye on their surroundings.

The first few moments of waiting were silent. The three of them were listening out for Moha's voice, waiting for him to storm through the building and for his voice to ring loudly. But nothing seemed to happen. The silence lingered on but it was soon broken by the harsh sound of a plate shattering on the floor.

"Where in the hells were you Xoco?" Moha yelled, his voice booming throughout the kitchen. Tacama clenched his fists tightly, worrying for his mother.

"You think you can just run off into the night? You'll get yourself killed, you fool!" Hitomi gritted her teeth and immediately reached for the door handle as rage was surging throughout her body. Tacama grabbed her dress and yanked her backwards, causing her to stumble.

"Wait!" He hissed whilst placing his hand around her mouth, preventing her from doing anything irrational. Astrid's heart was pounding heavily in her chest, frightened that something terrible was going to happen. But she needed to remain calm and composed.

"My apologies my lord!" Xoco cried out. "I was praying."

"Praying?" Moha growled in confusion.

"Yes sir, praying for my daughter, it is her birthday."

Hitomi, Astrid, and Tacama all looked at each other in surprise. Tacama looked extremely puzzled, wondering why his mother had referred to Izel, who had been dead for years.

"Have you forgotten that your daughter is *dead*! You're pathetic!" Moha shouted and threw pots and plates in Xoco's direction, all of them crashing down like thunder. Astrid and Hitomi looked at Tacama, wondering if they should do something now. Tacama nodded and grabbed his sword.

"Now." He whispered. Both Astrid and Hitomi reached for their blades. All three of them ran for the door with Astrid kicking it open.

"Stop this now, brother!" Tacama barked as Moha raised a hand to slap Xoco across the cheek. He stopped midway and looked at the trio, his jaw dropping. His eyes now displayed a sense of rage that none of them had witnessed before.

"What do you think you are doing here?" Moha growled, turning to his brother.

"The sun has risen, Moha," Tacama said sternly as he gripped his sword tightly, "and I have waited in silence for too long."

Moha stood back and let out a hearty laugh. He then began to clap slowly, mocking their attempts of storming in.

"I am *very impressed* little brother. Truly, I am." He roared. "Bringing mummy and the two lost princesses to fight alongside you? How adorable."

Astrid became infuriated at his taunts, treating them like fools. She muttered a curse beneath her breath and said in a low tone, "If we were playing, we would have brought dolls in place of blades."

"You expect me to fight a band of misfits?" Moha grinned as he looked back at his brother. "I must say that you make an *impressive* army between the three of you. The cowardly prince, the orphan, and the little brat. Do you even know what you've gotten yourselves into?'"

As the adrenaline surged through her body, Astrid felt courageous and bellowed out to Moha, "Do you ever shut up? You should have known that someone would stand up to you and put an end to your tyranny."

Moha let out another laugh and grabbed his dagger from his waist. "I've never seen you so riled up like this princess. It's invigorating! You want to fight, little one? Then come and strike me!" He yelled.

"Now Hitomi!" Tacama yelled abruptly. Hitomi began to run for Moha and was followed by Tacama. Xoco quickly stepped back and grabbed two knives beside her on the table while Astrid activated her Azuli sword. Tacama attacked first, swinging his sword at his brother's head while Hitomi aimed at his waist. Astrid leapt onto the table, making herself a clear target. Moha dodged both blows and before his mother attacked, he pushed Hitomi towards her and grabbed one of Xoco's blades. He turned towards Astrid and threw his dagger at her. Astrid hurled herself from the table and rolled onto the floor. She noticed that the obsidian blade had ricocheted off the wall and lay a few inches behind her. She began to reach for it before Moha noticed.

Tacama knew they were outmatched. He had underestimated his brother, he had become much stronger than before. His plan was beginning to fall apart. Even though they had the element of surprise at this moment, Tacama knew that it would be too dangerous to continue. He refused to let Hitomi and Astrid get hurt. Suddenly, Astrid was gesturing to him that she was now in possession of the key. That was their main priority and now that Astrid had the blade, they could escape while they still had a chance. Although they had vowed to help him, Tacama couldn't see himself letting these children die on his account.

"Astrid, Hitomi!" He yelled out, striking his brother and

preventing him from unsheathing his sword. "Get out of here, now! Take the dagger and run!"

Hitomi blocked another blow from Moha and dropped onto the floor, rolling underneath the table and managing to reach Astrid. Moha knew that he couldn't let Astrid and Hitomi leave, not when they were in possession of his blade. He leapt towards the table to grab hold of Hitomi, but his attempts were futile.

"We can handle this!" Tacama barked again, "Get out of here, now!"

Hitomi grabbed Astrid's arm and pulled her towards the door. Astrid couldn't leave Tacama and Xoco alone to fight Moha. Would she really allow them to die for her sake? She felt the need to dash back to their side and help. But Astrid knew she couldn't be so naive. She could tell from Moha's strength and skills that they were no match against him. With minimal fighting skills, she knew it would be smarter to let Xoco and Tacama fight this battle. She only hoped that they would make it out alive. She didn't want to lose them.

Astrid followed Hitomi outside and they quickly ran down the dirt road. Hitomi quickly caught sight of Xoco's secret route and dragged Astrid by the hand. Astrid remained hesitant, her feet refusing to carry on. Hitomi was trying her best to move Astrid, as if she was suddenly weighed down by a ton of bricks.

Before Astrid could say anything, there was a sharp sound that brought everything to complete silence. It sounded like lightning had struck the ground they stood on. They both knew that the sound came from the house. She had never heard such an ear-piercing noise before. Hitomi and Astrid stopped in their tracks and looked back in fear of what might have happened.

"Do you think that was them?" Hitomi whispered, catching her breath.

Astrid's heart sank and she began to fear for the worst. Her whole body froze, unable to move or think beyond the noise. She desperately wanted to go back but she had soon remembered what Tacama had told her just before they left to fight Moha.

'If I tell either one of you to run, you run. If you think Xoco or I are in danger you get out of there. Your safety is important, more important than getting the key.'

Swallowing hard, Astrid turned away from the house and took Hitomi's hand, whispering to her "We need to get out of here… They're fine. I know it." As they ran, Astrid began to cry. But she fought back her tears.

Disloyal to One,
Faithful to the Other

Instead of carrying on along the secret route, Hitomi and Astrid waited behind a row of barrels for Xoco and Tacama. But with every second that went by, worry began to flood their minds.

"We should go back Astrid. I don't like this." Hitomi whispered, wiping beads of sweat from her forehead. "What if they're hurt? Are we just going to let them die in there?" Astrid sighed and sat on the grass, feeling completely useless.

"I don't know," she whispered, burying her face in her hands. She wanted to go back, she knew she couldn't just let Tacama and Xoco die but she promised Tacama that she'd leave when he told her to. Astrid knew he wouldn't want to see Hitomi or herself killed just for his sake. Hitomi sat beside Astrid and put her arm around her. They both waited in silence.

"Are either of you injured?" Came a panicked voice from behind Astrid. The girls jumped and turned around, Hitomi grabbing her sword beside her. To their relief, it was Xoco.

Her face was filled with worry and her whole body was shaking. She placed her hand on Astrid's shoulder, noticing that she was distressed. Even though she had just endured a battle with her own son, she was still concerned for their well-being. Without thinking, Astrid leaped from the ground and embraced Xoco tightly.

"Oh Gods! Where were you? Are you hurt?" She gripped

Xoco tightly. Hitomi grabbed Astrid by the shoulder and pulled her away.

"Give her some space Astrid. I Thought you were going to suffocate her."

Xoco chuckled under her breath and simply nodded, saying, "I'm fine girls, I'll be just fine." She suddenly paused and started to look around in a distressed manner. A look of fear began to spread across her face. "Where's Tacama?" She whispered, frantically looking at the girls for an answer.

"We thought he was with you." Hitomi said. Xoco squeezed her eyes shut and cupped her hands to her mouth, quietly moaning in distress.

"What happened?" Muttered Astrid.

Regaining composure, Xoco sighed and said, "I was injured - barely - and it wouldn't have been safe to continue fighting. To make matters worse, a guard was approaching. I needed to stop him before he called more attention. I had lost track of Tacama and Moha when I returned. In an attempt to find them, I was confronted by another guard. I acted quickly and struck him on the chest. More guards were entering upon hearing the noise. I had no choice but to flee. I barely made it out of the house without being caught. I was hoping that Tacama had managed to find a way out." She looked fearfully back at the house.

"Should we wait for him here?" Hitomi asked. "He can't be too far away... right?"

Xoco let out a frustrated breath, already knowing that Tacama wouldn't be joining them anytime soon. She said in a low tone, "No, no we go to the rendezvous point. If he isn't there, then we mustn't go looking for him. He'll be handling the situation."

"Rendezvous point?" Astrid asked. "You never told us about a rendezvous point."

"Of course I didn't," Xoco snapped, her eyes now

looking stern. "You wouldn't go even if I told you where it was. I knew you'd stay hidden and wait for either myself or Tacama to come and find you. We are going to my brother's house. He is a spy for me who keeps an eye on Moha. But you may remember him from the 'coronation'. I know how he treated you that day, which is why Tacama and I knew you would refuse to go." Astrid crossed her arms in confusion.

"What do you mean?" She asked sternly.

"Cacama. He is Moha's right-hand man but he is also my little brother. All that you heard at the coronation was just gibberish so that Moha wouldn't suspect anything. He can keep us hidden for now and his daughter is a doctor, she'll patch us up and make sure we are fed."

Astrid was astonished. *Cacama? That grotesque pig was Xoco's brother! They didn't even look alike.* She grit her teeth at the thought of facing him again. The fact that Xoco is related to him was hard for Astrid to imagine. His skills of deception definitely paid off as Astrid truly felt that he was another minion of Moha's.

"Are you sure we can trust this guy?" Hitomi asked in a skeptical tone, "I mean, if he's with Moha."

"He's not *with* Moha!" Xoco hissed, trying not to raise her voice. "And yes, we can trust him. He is my brother. Tacama should be there as well."

They were both shocked in hearing Xoco getting annoyed. They knew that it would be useless to argue with her. Astrid knew there was no alternative but to face Cacama again and so she agreed and let Xoco lead the way.

Cacama and his daughter lived in a mud hut in the center of town. You couldn't tell which was his as it was hidden amongst the various huts and tents. It was like trying to find a needle in a haystack. The town was lively and busy, every corner hosting a stall of scents and jewels, the people were busily doing something. As they approached his hut,

Xoco let out an exasperated sigh and knocked on the door. Despite the trust she had in her brother, she wasn't too keen on seeing him either. Something shuffled behind the door and they were soon met by a young woman who was short and slender. A big smile appeared across her face which caused her large nose to crinkle at the bridge.

"Aunt Xoco!" She exclaimed in excitement and hugged Xoco around the neck. Xoco pulled away after a moment and placed a kiss on her niece's small forehead.

"Tepin, it is good to see you. How are you?" She opened the door wider for Xoco to come in.

"I'm great!" She said, grinning once more. Tepin noticed the distraction in her aunt's eyes as Xoco looked around the house in an agitated manner.

"Is Tacama here at all?" Xoco muttered.

Tepin sighed gently and said, "Sorry, but I haven't seen him. Is he alright? Has something happened?"

"Nothing, he was just..." Xoco sighed and looked at Hitomi and Astrid beside her.

"It doesn't matter. He should be here shortly. Is your father here?" She asked gently.

Tepin scoffed and said, "Well of course, but he's being cranky. I'd come back later if I were you Aunt Xoco, father's being very stubborn."

"No, no it's fine. I told him I was coming."

"Well I warned you." Said Tepin as she moved out of the way from the door.

"Come in."

The three of them entered the hut and slipped off their shoes one by one beside the door. As Hitomi and Astrid entered, Tepin looked shocked at seeing them. The people of Tolico have never encountered individuals who were different, who clearly didn't belong to the island. Tepin simply stared at them in surprise, as if she had seen the gods walk through her door.

"Please don't stare." Hitomi growled as she walked past Tepin. Astrid tried to nudge Hitomi for snapping at Tepin.

Astrid smiled at their host and introduced herself. "My name is Astrid," she said, turning to Tepin, "I'm a friend of X…"

"Yes I know." Tepin muttered crossing her arms, "It's just interesting to finally meet the girl that Xoco has been talking about for years, that's all." Astrid realized Tepins mistake and went to grab Hitomi but she had already walked away towards Xoco.

"Oh, I'm not her, that's Hitomi. I've only been here for a few days." Astrid said immediately. Tepin didn't look amused at hearing this. She simply walked towards the others, leaving Astrid to scurry on behind. She noticed that this hut was quite spacious despite its size. As she approached the others, a familiar voice was soon heard.

"Tepin, here is the one your aunt was speaking of last night, the princess of Egypt." Cacama was sitting on the other side of the room and as soon as he saw Astrid, he rose from his seat, standing a few feet away from Astrid. It was as if Astrid was looking at a different person.

His posture was more relaxed than it was at the coronation and his face was also relaxed, wearing a smile that was genuine. Cacama walked over to his sister but a form of discomfort lingered on his face. He didn't make an attempt to hug her as his daughter had and Xoco made no attempt either. You wouldn't believe that they were brother and sister from their distant behavior.

"It's nice to see you again." Cacama said in a monotone voice. He then noticed her injuries and looked over to Tepin, simply saying, "Tepin, tend to your aunt's wounds. They look like they need much attention." It was surprising that no one had noticed the severity of her injuries. The blood had managed to seep through the thick fabric of her dress, staining her shoulder crimson. Astrid and Hitomi looked at each other briefly, wondering how they had managed to miss that.

As Tepin ushered Xoco to the other side of the room so that she could treat her, Cacamas relaxed persona soon shifted into an uncomfortable and rigid stance. He seemed to be the most nervous person in the room.

Perhaps he was hiding something from the others. Astrid was still finding it hard to trust him after seeing his display during the coronation. Looking at Xoco and Cacama, Astrid found it strange that they both tried to avoid as much contact with each other as possible. Neither of them seemed to look at the other, they acted like neither of them were even in the room. Astrid thought about this for a moment whilst Tepin talked about what Xoco had told her of the foreign princesses. It was strange being referred to in the third person.

After the small-talk had ceased between them, the room was soon filled with overwhelming silence that couldn't be ignored. But Astrid knew the main focus of everyone's minds – whether or not Tacama was safe and if he would rejoin them. The more Astrid thought about it, the more she regretted not going back for him and as the silence continued, she felt her chest beginning to tighten with anxiety.

Tacama had made it perfectly clear that he wouldn't let anyone die for him but it didn't make them feel any better when they knew that he could be in serious danger out there. Astrid understood that Tacama would have been guilt-stricken if she had died but she felt that his life was as equally important as her own. Even though they had made an oath to the death to protect Tolico and the realms, it felt like their rebellion had come to an abrupt end.

Checkmate

Feeling weak and broken, Tacama still fought, ignoring the pain that surged through his body. He was starting to clutch at straws. Looking around to see what he could use against Moha, he grabbed hold of a wooden chair and swung it over Moha's head. Despite his efforts, Moha blocked the blow with his forearm, grabbing it fiercely and then threw it to the floor. It broke apart abruptly, half of it splintered and ruined.

Moha looked deranged, fueled on nothing but his hatred for Tacama. He yelled out in a demented tone, "You think a *chair* can stop me *brother*?" Moha roared in rage as he struck his blade against Tacama's knees. The blade struck deep, causing Tacama to keel over. Blood was dripping from the wound and the pain was excruciating.

Even though his body was searing with agony, Tacama wasn't going to give up just yet. He was done with the small talk, he had waited fourteen years for this fight and he wasn't going to lose because of Moha's wit and strength. He dug his blade into the ground and pushed himself upwards, causing his wounded leg to shake uncontrollably.

Moha stood by and taunted him, waving his sword above him and yelling at him to get off his ass and fight. Catching him off guard, Tacama struck his brother's sword, causing Moha to drop the weapon. Realizing that he had been left exposed, Moha scrabbled for the sword. But before he could reach it, Tacama drove his blade deeply into his brothers' shoulder.

Blood oozed around the metal of the sword. Moha cried

out in pain as Tacama yanked his blade from his brother's arm while Moha grabbed hold of his bloodied shoulder, his hand quickly covered in blood.

"A chair may not defeat you!" Yelled Tacama as he swung his sword towards Moha's face, "But a blade never fails." Tacama growled as he kicked his brothers' sword across the room and out of reach.

Moha let out a monstrous howl as he shot a lethal glare at his brother. Tacama could see the fear in Moha's eyes; there was no escape for him. But that didn't mean that Moha was going to give up. If he couldn't fight with a sword, then he would find an alternative. One tactic that Tacama didn't count on was the cruelty of Moha's words.

"You really think you can kill me?" Moha hissed. "What are you trying to accomplish Tacama? Are you going to *protect* the people you care about, again? Ha! You know what happened last time! I promise you that it will happen again!" Moha stepped back, now leaning against the wall and he shook the sweat from his hair.

The blood loss from his shoulder was taking its toll on Moha, he began to shake and his skin was becoming paler. But he still managed to conjure up a demented smile and he continued to torture Tacama with his plot of cruelty.

"Well, what you do not know is that a special friend of mine is out there right now, scouring the town for mother and the *little lost princesses*."

Oh gods, Tacama thought. *He's sent an assassin!* Moha licked his lips and his grin now stretched from cheek to cheek.

"I had no such luck in finding them. But don't worry, they'll be brought here shortly. Who better to send out than the man who had taken them in the first place. So it looks like you've failed again brother. I'm so sorry."

"You..." Tacama whispered through gritted teeth. He was now filled with fear and anger. He could no longer take control of the anger that was building up within him and with the force of a hundred men, he drove his sword up and swung it towards Moha once more, yelling, "You monster!"

Moha knew he was outmatched. He saw the power and skill within Tacama, seeing what he was capable of when he didn't hold back. However, he knew that if Tacama wasn't holding back anymore, then neither would he.

Before Tacama could strike, Moha said to Tacama in a mocking tone, "Is this what father would want, Tacama?" Moha seethed and gripped his wounded shoulder.

"Would he really want you seeking out revenge on your own brother?"

Tacama gripped his sword tighter; he wouldn't let Moha beat him now, especially without a weapon. These were just feeble words that Moha was throwing around as a final attempt to beat him.

"This isn't revenge Moha. I am avenging my family, our family!" Tacama yelled. Moha let out a weak chuckle whilst admiring the wounds he had carved into his brother.

"Our family?" He hissed. "Oh no brother, they were never my family. They were all yours. They were nothing but hindrances in my path, trying to deter me from my main objective. And now I've met it, I have seen all of those girls and boys with pretty blue eyes and now they are gone. It was like squashing a bug, one by one. A priest told me as a child that these people were made because the gods wanted us humans to change, to survive. Well, who's surviving now?"

Even though Moha had slaughtered his family, Tacama had never truly hated him during the past fourteen years he had spent in the pyramid.

But at this moment, Tacama finally felt truly betrayed. Moha had denied their existence and acted like they were mere pawns in his game. He was pretending to be a mighty god but he was nothing more than a wild dog. Just as Moha had abandoned his family, Tacama was going to abandon Moha. In that moment, Moha was nothing more than a stray animal to Tacama, filled with disease and hatred and it was now Tacama's job to put this poor dog down.

Who's surviving now? Tacama thought as he stared at the man he once considered his brother, the man he had spent years playing with, fighting with, loving... but now this man meant nothing to him. He thought about the options that were left for Tacama; he could leave Moha here to bleed out or he could make it quick and end it. No matter what decision Tacama made, he would laugh at his ironic last words. *Who's surviving now?*

Tacama had made up his mind. In an instant he lifted his sword, pointed the tip at Moha's heart and drove it through his chest, hearing the bones crunch beneath his blade. As blood began to gush from this new wound, Moha gripped the sharp steel in his hand and tried to remove it. But Tacama held firm twisting the sword as he stared into the eyes of the man who had killed his family.

"Who's surviving now my brother?... Not you, definitely not you."

"He should be here by now." Cacama said abruptly as he stood from his chair. "I wouldn't be surprised if Moha has killed him," he said in a low tone.

"Don't say that!" Cried Xoco. "He's fine!"

Cacama glared at Xoco, wondering why she was trying to pretend that everything was alright. He then stared at his daughter, as if waiting for her to say something to Xoco. Seeing how everyone had fallen silent, Cacama decided that something needed to be done. He grabbed his robe from his chair, fastening it securely around himself and he walked toward the back door.

Before he left, he looked at Xoco and said in a low tone,

"Xoco, your son is either in danger, or he's *dead*. Either way, we can't just simply wait here and hope for the best. I am going after him. Tepin, you will take the girls and Aunt Xoco home and make sure you are not seen. I will meet with you shortly."

Xoco wrenched Cacama's shoulder tightly and said to him sternly, "You think I'm going to let you go after Tacama *alone*?"

Cacama stared at Xoco, annoyed that she was delaying him from finding his nephew. Realizing that she wasn't going to loosen her grip without a compromise, he sighed heavily and said, "Damn you Xoco, I'll be perfectly safe out there, no one will question my presence at the palace. They all see me as Moha's royal guard dog, too frightened to even come within an inch of my presence. If you go, you could get yourself killed! How would Tacama feel if he knew that I let you go out there and you were killed?"

Xoco paused, thinking about what could happen if she left Astrid and Hitomi but what would also happen if she simply waited and let her brother go. She looked up at Cacama, her face filled with great annoyance as she knew that he was right.

She released her grip and whispered, "Make sure you bring him back to me."

The room went silent. Astrid and Hitomi were on the edge of their seats, wondering if Xoco would go back and face Moha again. Astrid's fingers were clamped onto the seat of her chair, her nails digging deeply into the frail wooden structure.

Cacama grit his teeth in an effort to hide his empathy towards his sister and he spat. "Damn it, Xoco, don't you understand? Moha is godlike with a sword; Tacama could be in pieces right now! You really want me to bring a bloody pile back to you?"

Xoco gasped and clamped her hand over her mouth. She

violently shook her head while choking on her own sobs. Hitomi almost leapt out of her seat in anger, tempted to slap Cacama's face in making Xoco cry. But she resisted temptation and remained seated, her face filled with anger.

"No! Don't you dare say that! You bring my son back to me, brother! *You bring him back*!" Xoco cried out.

Cacama let out a heavy sigh and shook his head slowly, questioning Xoco's optimism. He then turned to Tepin and said, "Get them out of here. Take them back to the forest and remain hidden within their hut. No one is to leave, you will wait for my return."

He pushed Xoco aside and left through the back door. As Tepin now had a job to fulfill, she rose from her seat and walked towards Xoco, taking hold of her arm.

"Come on, we need to go. Let's go outside." Tepin whispered to Xoco. She similarly gave the same message to Astrid and Hitomi, telling them to get ready to leave. Hitomi remained dubious about Tepin but she simply didn't like to be treated like an infant. She reluctantly followed Tepin and Xoco out of the house, holding her sword firmly at the hilt.

But Astrid paused at the door, her mind still consumed with the thought of Tacama being in severe danger. She swallowed hard and looked back, wondering how Cacama was going to save Tacama.

"I forgot my cape," she called out to the others, hoping no one would notice that she was still wearing her robe. Being preoccupied with the others, Tepin told Astrid to be quick. Seizing the moment, Astrid closed the door behind her and walked towards the main room.

As she entered, she noticed that Cacama had gathered together an assortment of swords and knives and placed them on a table, deciding on which weapon would be the most efficient.

Too preoccupied with the swords, he didn't even seem

to notice that Astrid was only a few inches behind him, or perhaps he was simply ignoring her. She walked closer towards Cacama, taking baby steps so that she wouldn't alarm him.

"Do you really think Tacama is dead?" She asked in a serious tone, her posture strong and firm. He didn't respond at first, acting as if he hadn't heard her. He grabbed a sharp knife, placing it into its sheath and then attaching it to his waist. He then gripped his fists tightly but he didn't make an attempt to look at Astrid.

"That's none of your business," he said in a hoarse tone. That had taken Astrid by surprise. What had she done to deserve such ill treatment? She wasn't going to stand by and let him speak to her in such a lowly manner.

"None of my business?" Astrid yelled and stomped her foot on the floor. She stormed around to his side, trying to look him in the eye while he simply stared at his weaponry.

"I know you think I'm weak Cacama, that I'm nothing more than a child but I am more than that. I've made an oath with Tacama and Hitomi, an oath to protect Tolico to the death. I haven't known Tacama as long as you have but I do care for him."

Cacama slammed his fist on the table and met Astrid with a sombre stare. His eyes were unrelenting, as if they could see into her mind.

"You shouldn't be involved with this! This isn't your kingdom and it isn't your business. You have no idea what's going on here in Tolico, so don't you dare tell me that you've come to protect this place. You don't know about the horrors that Moha has committed, if you knew what he has done you would to be far away from this damned island. We don't want your help here. What can a little girl like you do for us? Moha is unstoppable. He's not human! He's a demon and no one can kill him, not even you little girl."

Astrid wanted to scream and slap him at the same time but she couldn't let her anger get the better of her. She realized that she needed to calm down rather than spout out meaningless words that would only make the situation worse.

She gathered her thoughts together and tried to think of something rational to say, but then let the first words that came to her mind flow out of her mouth.

"I already know what has happened here. You think I'd join a rebellion and risk my life for a cause that I knew nothing about? Tacama told me everything about his father, how he traveled to distant lands and fought for the weak. You may say that Tolico doesn't need help but I feel that this island needs all the help it can get. Your people have grown to fear Moha, to obey him through terror. You claim he is a demon? He is a mere living being like the rest of us and all living things must die. I can imagine that Tolico wasn't always like this, a destitute land under the rule of a madman. I have been brought here against my will, the least I can do is to somehow resolve this problem. But above all else, I need to know if Tacama is alive, I need to know if my army will be one man short."

"I don't know." Cacama roared out. Any sense of sanity immediately vanished in that moment. Astrid was finally able to see the true side of Cacama, a man who is simply frightened for his family. "I don't know if Tacama is alive, Astrid. The last time I saw him with a blade was when he was just a boy and he could barely hold it. But I know for a fact that Moha's sword fighting skills are incredible and yet unnatural. If you know so much about what happened to Tacama's family, then you should know that Tacama has no chance. They were slaughtered. You're only making this situation worse and you're being stupid and naive. You can't help, and I'm not being arrogant when I say that, I truly mean it. There's no way to stop that monster. Xoco told me you had a way home but you refused? Why would you do that? But that doesn't matter, you've practically thrown your chance away because Tacama is as good as dead. You're being reckless and stupid. I do hope you're happy now, you've managed to get yourself stuck on this forsaken island and you will die here."

"The fact that I remain hopeful towards this cause does not mean that I am stupid. People who sit by and have nothing but fear to cling to are the stupid ones." Astrid exclaimed as she slammed her hands onto the table, trying to regain eye contact with Cacama once again, leaning over to see if there was even the slightest glimmer of hope left in him. "Whether you like it or not, this war involves us all, including me." Astrid said sternly.

He mumbled under his breath and turned away from Astrid, placing focus on a sword he had grabbed from the table.

Astrid sighed, knowing that Cacama would refuse to understand. "I suppose we have already lost the war if we refuse to fight for the cause," she said in a final effort to change his mind.

She slowly walked away from the table, feeling that she hadn't done enough to change his mind. Suddenly, the sharp sound of a sword clanging against the ground made her come to a halt. She instantly turned around. His posture changed ever so slightly. Something in Cacama snapped.

"What did you just say to me?" His voice rumbled in the back of his throat and he gripped the edge of the table, digging his nails deeply into the wood.

Despite the seething anger of a man who was twice the size of a young girl, Astrid stood her ground and said in a harsh tone, "What I meant to say is that I feel sorry for those few people who choose to cower away in fear of Moha and whimper like a dog. But I want to help them stand up to tyranny."

She could feel Cacama seething with rage from across the room and it was evident that he was trying to hold back but it didn't last long. She could hear his nails scratching into the table. Astrid knew she had gone too far now. She swallowed her fear and clenched her hands into fists by her sides. *Gods help me.*

"I refuse to seek help from a child!" He bellowed and he instantly grabbed a dagger beside him. Turning around swiftly, he threw the dagger at Astrid.

Before Astrid could even move, the dagger abruptly stopped in mid-air, hovering just an inch from her eye. It soon dropped to the floor, clanging against the ground. They both remained still, unable to believe what their eyes had just seen.

It's as if they were both frozen, unable to move a single muscle. Beads of sweat decorated Astrid's forehead. She could feel her mouth hanging wide open at the shock and she looked over to Cacama to see his reaction. His eyes had doubled in size and fear petrified his face as he stared at the dagger.

"You did that," he whispered and finally looked back up at Astrid.

She didn't know how to respond to that. She wasn't aware about any special powers. Her parents never mentioned anything to her about unnatural abilities. She began to doubt herself for a second, wondering if she had been in the sun for too long.

Did that really just happen? She wondered if the gods were watching over her and had blessed her with a special gift. But that was a bit difficult for Astrid to take in.

Tacama stepped down from his horse and took in a deep breath at the sight of the palace. It hadn't been properly used since the death of Tacama's father and he couldn't understand why it was still occupied by servants. It was as if they had been waiting for the king's arrival. Perhaps the wait was finally over.

Tacama pushed his way through a group of people and made his way to the main doors. He placed his hand on the large spiral handle and his heart skipped a beat. The last time he touched this door was fourteen years ago. The people on this island have endured fourteen years of being governed by a demon and for Tacama, it has been fourteen years of hiding away like a coward.

Not anymore. Tacama thought and he decided in that moment that he would never hide again.

He pulled open the doors and walked into his home. With every step he took, more memories of that day came flooding back, memories of finding his sister, his wife and his child dead. A part of him wanted nothing more than to run away from the memories, from this palace, but he couldn't. He had begun a war and now he had to finish it.

The main hall was empty but Tacama could hear that people were nearby. He had to get their attention somehow. Now was his chance, now he had to play pretend like an actor on a stage.

He took in a deep breath and formed a terrified look on his face before calling out in a frail and frightened voice, "The king! The king has been hurt!"

All at once, knights and servants came billowing out of every door with panic in their voices. Many of the maids shrieked at the site of Tacama who was still bloodied and battered.

Through the large crowd came a tall wide man wearing a full suit of armor, Tacama assuming that this must have been Moha's personal knight. Tacama swallowed hard as if he was out of breath and rushed to the man.

"Who are you? What about the king?" The knight growled and gripped Tacama's shoulders firmly. Tacama pretended to be absolutely frantic and implored this knight for help.

"I am prince Tacama. I was with my brother in his private quarters! An assassin came and attacked the king! I barely made it out... Oh Gods forgive me! I was unable to save our king!" Now was the final piece. Tacama held his hands to his face, he began to moan gently and in a strained voice, he whispered, "King Moha... is dead."

The entire hall gasped simultaneously. The knight seemed to turn from a strong man to a tiny boy within seconds.

"Dead...?" he muttered. Tacama nodded in confirmation.

"What are we to do?" Cried out a servant from the crowd. Tacama let out a heavy breath and spoke out loudly for all to hear.

"I cannot retrieve our king's body, for he has been butchered by the beast of an assassin. The only thing I have left of him is the blood on my clothes."

"You can do more than that, your highness," the knight said as he stepped back from Tacama. Tacama looked up in a form of fake surprise.

The knight looked from Tacama to the crowd and gave a solemn nod. "You are the last member of the royal family." Looking upon the crowd, the knight announced, "Tolico cannot live without a rightful ruler upon the throne." He went down on one knee and bowed his head to Tacama, "You are now King of Tolico. Long live the King."

The servants and guards behind the knight followed his actions and bowed to their new king, chanting the phrase, "Long live the King."

Tacama hid a smile and nodded in silence, as though being king was an unwanted burden. He looked upon the crowd of people that were now chanting for him.

Finally, after fourteen years, Tolico was out of harm's way.

Regis Sicarius

"I didn't do anything!" Astrid yelled but Cacama didn't seem to hear any of it. He only stared blankly at her, still completely petrified. "Why won't you say anything! Answer me!" Astrid repeated and finally caught his attention but not in the way she had expected.

"Fight the war." Cacama choked out. "Do it."

Before Astrid could conjure up a reply, Hitomi, Xoco and Tepin, wondering where Astrid had disappeared to, returned.

"What's taking so long?" Tepin paused at her father's expression and looked to Astrid for an answer. All three of them were confused upon seeing these two facing each other from a distance. After a moment, Cacama finally responded to his daughter.

"I was asking her a few questions about Tacama." He sputtered before turning back to the table, gathering a case of blades and turning to leave. "I'm sorry I took so long." And swiftly he left.

"What was that all about?" Hitomi asked. Astrid glanced down at the dagger that was still stuck in the floorboards, only a few inches from her feet.

On hearing Hitomi's question, she gently said, "I don't know." The girls soon made their way back into the forest after parting ways with Cacama. Astrid had remained silent since they left the hut whilst everyone else had begun talking about Tacama.

Astrid couldn't find the strength to speak, she was so confused and her mind was racing faster than a horse. She desperately wanted to talk to someone about what had just happened back in the hut. But who could she talk to? Astrid wanted answers, but she knew that no one would be able to explain what had happened to her. Astrid was wondering if this ability was a curse rather than a blessing.

"Wait". Hitomi's voice cut short Astrid's train of thought. She looked up at the others ahead of her to see what was going on. Tepin, Xoco and Hitomi were all standing still, staring farther into the forest, they remained frozen in place.

"What is it?" Astrid muttered as she stepped closer to them. When none of them replied she looked at their expressions for any sort of clue. Tepin's face was the most peculiar. There was something within her confused expression that made it seem as though her focus was on something else.

Her eyes were downcast but she didn't appear to be looking at anything in particular. Perhaps her mind was trying to focus on something else. At last, Tepin snapped out of her trance-like state and looked forward, trying to see something in the distance.

"Do you hear that?" She whispered, looking at the others for confirmation.

Astrid strained to hear it but it seemed that Xoco and Hitomi already knew what it was as Hitomi said, "Someone's whistling."

Astrid tried to concentrate her hearing on the sound, but the only thing that flooded her ears was the sound of birds singing in the distance. The whistling came to an abrupt stop.

"I don't hear it anymore," said Hitomi in surprise. "Do you?"

Suddenly, the whistling started up again, but this time it was much closer. Then, from a mountain of bushes in front of the group came the crisp sound of crunching leaves.

Hitomi grabbed the hilt of her sword, ready to unsheathe it at any moment. She looked towards the others and made a gesture to them to prepare themselves. Xoco was prepared with a dagger whilst she stood slightly in front of Tepin. Astrid stepped back and gripped onto her Azuli sword. They waited for the stranger to emerge. Was it a person or an animal that would leap out at them?

"How adorable! Three little girls and an old woman, all so eager to play with blades. Ha!" The bushes moved once more and suddenly something arose from the flora.

The mysterious being unfolded at the waist and its arms were outstretched from its back. It soon equipped itself with a sword in each hand. This figure was swift in movement, moving as smoothly as smoke. "I could kill you all now but I would love to see you 'fight'... and lose."

The voice belonged to the figure of a full grown man whose skin was a slightly darker in complexion than theirs and he was by far the tallest man that they had ever seen. Hitomi cast her own sword upwards and took a battle stance.

"Who are you?" Yelled Tepin, rolling her bare hands into fists.

The man burst into laughter. "Who am I?" He barked. "Who am *I*? Well to you two," he nodded towards Tepin and Xoco, "you are nothing. However, to the two blue-eyed girls, I have been assigned to take you both to the palace. But to be more personal, my name is Acalan."

That name rang a bell within Astrid's head. She had heard that name before. She then remembered who it belonged to. Astrid's heart beat rapidly, feeling as if it would break free from her chest.

'Take her to the boat Acalan, do whatever you want with her, just keep her alive.'

The man who had taken her was standing in front of her now. He had returned, and this time, he would either take them back to the palace or he would eliminate them both. Astrid knew that this was Moha's doing. But did that mean that Moha had escaped from Tacama and had now sent Acalan to kill them both. Or perhaps Tacama was killed by Moha.

She couldn't dwell on that thought. What mattered right now was finding a way to stop Acalan. If he had really come to kill her and Hitomi, then Astrid had to do something about it. She hadn't come all this way just for someone to kill her now.

"Xoco, Tepin, get back! He doesn't want either of you." She yelled out, turning back to the two of them.

Acalan chuckled under his breath and he stepped out from the brush.

"Look at you, being so brave." He gripped his swords tighter. "We'll have to change that."

Xoco pushed herself in front of Astrid and Hitomi and raised her small dagger towards Acalan. She pushed them both towards Tepin, who held them back from Xoco.

"No you won't!" She yelled, diminishing any signs of weakness that she had from before. She stood strong in front of the assassin, showing no signs of fear from his intimidating stature or weaponry.

"I think you should put your little dagger away now and leave. I'm being polite which is very rare so I think you should leave now woman!" He roared at Xoco, trying to make her waver from her stance. He then began to snigger at Xoco's determination, his expression grew harder and he rolled his head back, belting out a laughter that sounded like that of a menacing hyena.

His tall stature made him look unnatural and eerie as his body moved fluently back and forth. He reached over Xoco's blade and clamped a hand on her shoulder.

"It's admirable that you think you could stand a chance against me. But who do you think you're fooling? Who do you think you are?"

Xoco yanked herself free from his grasp and blocked his way from the girls, proudly stating, "I am the former queen of Tolico, Queen Xoco. You may think I'm nothing more than a an old woman. But I promise you, if you hurt my girls, I will kill you."

"Xoco, stop this!" Astrid barked, running up to her. "He isn't here to hurt you, he's here for me."

"Shut up, Astrid," said Tepin from behind her as she grabbed her arm and pulled her back. "We're not leaving you. If this assassin wants to kill you and Hitomi, then he has to get though Xoco and me." She stood in front of them both, crossed her arms over her chest and smiled at Acalan, saying to him confidently, "You understand, boy?"

Acalan bit down on his lip and cackled, "Oh I understand perfectly."

Moving quickly like lightning, he swung one sword towards Xoco and Tepin and another towards Astrid and Hitomi. Astrid activated her Azuli sword and swung it upwards to block the edge of Acalan's weapon from hitting Hitomi.

"Stop this now!" She screamed, shoving his blade down towards the grass. "If you came here to kill me, then go ahead and try. You weren't assigned to kill Xoco or Tepin, so don't. Come and fight the person you were assigned to. If I were up against you a few weeks ago, I would be dead. But now, I think I can take you on. And to add to that, I'm in a very bad mood so I will cut you down."

Acalan sighed, looking shocked but amazed at the same time. He gave a slight nod to Astrid. But this amazement was short lived.

"Women," he scoffed. "Throwing a fit every time there's blood between your legs."

Ughh! How disgusting! Astrid grit her teeth and raised her Azuli sword as she looked every bit the warrior. She may not have had as much training as a man would have, but she was confident that she could at least disable Acalan. She had 'fought' him once, perhaps she could do it again.

"Perhaps you'll be happy to hear that your employer, Moha, is dead! And I helped in ending him. I wouldn't be surprised if you wet yourself right now." Astrid grinned.

She knew that there was a chance that Moha was alive but it was the only card that she could use. It seemed to work in her favor from the look of it. Acalan simply scoffed at the statement, trying to remain composed and undeterred. But Astrid could tell that she'd caught him off guard.

It felt as though everything in the forest had fallen silent upon hearing Astrid's words. The sound of the wind through the trees couldn't even be heard. Hitomi, Xoco and Tepin were proud of Astrid for having such courage, but they now worried for how Acalan would react to this piece of 'news'.

Astrid couldn't tell if she had made matters worse as Acalan now possessed a stare that made her body shake to the core. He rose up once again, not wasting time on any words she might use.

"So, if you want to fight me, the killer of the king," Astrid said, cutting through the quietness with the sharpness of her blade. "Then go ahead."

Tacama burst into his uncle's home and called out to see if they were there. With no reply, he looked around the main room, looking for any trace of them. He stepped forward toward Cacama's worktable, his heart beating as fast. He feared the worst had happened.

Oh gods, I'm too late. He closed his eyes, taking in a deep breath and wiped away the beads of sweat from his face. However, as he walked towards the table, something had pricked the tip of his toes. It was cool and smooth.

Tacama looked down to find a dagger stuck in the floor. This looked like one of his uncle's daggers, but why was it on the floor? His heart momentarily stopped, fearing that the assassin had already arrived. Had Cacama tried to fight against the assassin or was he overpowered.

Tacama stooped down, picking the delicate dagger from the floor he inspected it. The blade was spotless, not a speck of blood in sight. Tacama felt relieved in knowing that no one had been injured, he felt like he could breathe again. But he remained troubled about why the blade was on the ground. His uncle is renowned for his throwing skills, he never missed his target. Although he had aged forty years from that title, Tacama knew that his uncle could easily hit an assassin with a blade like this.

Even though Tacama assumed that his uncle and the others were safe, he wondered where they were now. This was the rendezvous point; it was a safe place. Where else could they have gone to? At first, his mind went blank but it soon came to him.

The shack! Hitomi's shack within the forest, no one knew where it was and anyone else would be too afraid to step foot within the timberland.

He was heading for his horse, but he soon realized that it would look suspicious if people saw the King of Tolico riding into the forest. So he decided to make his way to the forest on foot, making sure no one would see him. He grabbed his cloak from the saddle of his horse and fastened it firmly around him. He put up his hood and began walking.

He reached the outskirts of the forest and then went into the gloom under the trees. Tacama soon had no idea which way to turn, every tree looked the same and he couldn't find the route that led to the shack. But what if the girls never reached the place? They might have been detained or captured.

Just as he journeyed deeper into the forest, something glinting a few inches from where he stood caught his attention. Tacama knelt down and moved the dead leaves away to reveal the object. It was small but bright. He picked it up, feeling the smoothness of it, it looked familiar.

It was the teardrop pendant. Its lapis surface was distinctive, making it hard to miss. Which meant that Astrid and Hitomi must be nearby. Hitomi knew how to cover her tracks while going in and out of the forest and she probably knew that Tacama would have been hopeless in trying to track them down without some sort of clue.

"Clever girls." He whispered as he clutched the pendant firmly to his chest.

Tacama continued walking quickly as he now knew that he was on the right track. But doubt plagued his mind, wondering whether or not they were safe. Suddenly, he heard something in the distance but he couldn't make out what it was. He thought the wind was trying to trick him, creating illusions from nothing. He tried to get closer to the source.

Instantly, the sounds of swords clashing became clearer and more distinct. He unsheathed his weapon and made his way quietly but with speed through the woods. He needed to know who was fighting in order to eliminate the possibility of it being Astrid, Hitomi or his mother. And it was also wise to investigate the skirmish, making sure to get a view of the enemy.

Concealing himself amongst the bushes, Tacama was able to catch sight of the fight. One of the swordsmen was a tall and bulky man, fighting with two long claymores and his opponent was Astrid.

Astrid! What has she gotten herself into? Tacama thought. *She's going to get herself killed!* Hitomi and Xoco were trying their best to block his strikes but he had managed to avoid their every move. It was clear that his focus was on Astrid.

Tacama saw Tepin standing a few feet away from the group with nothing to defend herself. She was looking around for something that she could use as a weapon. Tacama took a gladius from his belt and moved slowly towards Tepin whilst trying to stay concealed behind the trees.

Standing a few feet from his cousin, he needed to find a way to get her attention without alerting the bulky swordsman. He began to mimic the sound of a Loon, hoping that Tepin would remember the tune from when they were younger. Cacama had taught them both how to mimic the calls of the native birds as children, telling them that it would be valuable in communicating with each other. Out of all of the calls, Tepin adored the call of the Loon. Tacama was hoping that she would still remember the call. *Come on Tepin. You know this sound.*

And she did.

Tepin perked her head up like a Loon itself, looking around for the source of the sound. She turned slightly towards the dense shrubbery and found Tacama's face amongst the woodland. Her face immediately lit up like the sun as she caught sight of him. Tacama held his finger to his lips, signaling Tepin to keep quiet. He threw the blade forward and it landed in front of her, with the tip of the blade firmly in the ground. He chirped once again to catch her attention before nodding towards Astrid.

"Wait here," he mouthed to her and gripped his sword tighter before heading forwards toward the others.

This had to be the assassin Moha had mentioned. Tacama thought. No ordinary brute who was looking for a fight would carry blades as large as his, planning for each strike to deal a deathly blow Tacama knew Astrid couldn't deal with this man alone, it would be a challenge for Tacama to deal with, let alone a young girl with little experience in sword fighting.

He could tell that Astrid was exhausted, her movements were getting slower with every strike he made. He promised Astrid that he wouldn't let her get hurt and he intended to keep it that way. He needed to get Astrid and Hitomi safely back to Egypt. He breathed in deeply and gripped his fingers tightly around the hilt of his blade.

"You choose to fight a child? How pathetic." Tacama barked and emerged from the forest wall. The assassin startled paused mid swing and glared at Tacama, a look of pure rage seared within his dark eyes.

"Who are you to judge, peasant?" He scoffed and stepped away from Astrid, who looked equally as shocked and terrified.

"Peasant? I'd be careful if I were you. You sure you want to talk to me like that?" Tacama chuckled. "I mean, you are talking to the King of Tolico after all. It is extremely rude to refer to your king as a peasant. I could kill you for that."

He pulled his sword from his waist, still stained with his brother's blood and pointed it at Acalan's neck.

Astrid was truly amazed. This man, who was intent on spilling her blood was put into his place like a dog. She had never seen someone so terrified and confused at the same time. By the gods, so much had happened within a number of seconds. All at once, she was filled with dread and hope and it made her stomach churn. But now wasn't the time for her to feel sick. Just because Tacama had arrived at the right moment, that didn't mean that everything was alright. Tacama's presence also didn't put her mind at ease. In fact, it made her feel even more confused.

"King?" Acalan growled. He lunged forwards, and grabbed the tip of the blade. He pushed it slightly forward, causing his hand to bleed severely. The blood dripped down the blade. He grit his teeth and brought it back to its original position. He then spat on the sword.

"Bullshit. You are no king to me. Moha shall live on forever! He is a god amongst men!"

Tacama let out a heavy, frustrated sigh and said, "No he is a mere mortal like everyone else. I have proof."

Acalan clenched his grip on the blade tighter, saying in a hoarse tone, "And what proof would that be?"

The assassin wasn't the only one awaiting Tacama's reply. Everyone waited in anticipation to hear what he was going to say.

Tacama looked up at Acalan and grinned. He then looked down at his sword, saying gently, "Take a look at the blade. His blood has stained it and so has yours." He looked down at the blade, noticing how his fresh flowing blood was now covering the dried up stains on the blade. He immediately pulled the sword back quickly, slicing deep into Acalan's fingers before guarding himself.

He stood frozen like a statue. His face looked lost, trying to figure out what had happened. His mind was elsewhere, leaving his body in shock and terror. He didn't even notice that his finger was almost severed and blood was pouring from the palm of his hand.

"You heard me," Tacama yelled. "He is dead. And, as a loyal servant of the king, you are now under *my* command."

"But... *How*?" Acalan asked, his voice cracking and his eyes downcast in shock. Tacama lowered his sword slightly, knowing that Acalan was in a docile state.

"As I said, Moha is a mere mortal. He was never a god." Then his face changed to a look of sympathy. "But he is now at peace. His spirit has been taken from this realm while his body remains here. He will never return."

Acalan dropped to his knees, both alarmed and confused. He had no choice but to trust what Tacama said, he was too shocked to do anything else. Tacama lowered his blade upon Acalan's shoulder.

"Now, I have not stepped foot into the town square of

Tolico in a very long time, but I do hear the words of its people. I have heard men, women and children chanting the same sentence over and over. 'Long live the king.' So, what do you think you should say to the king of Tolico?"

The assassin raised his head, his eyes looking lost like a child.

"Long live the king," he whispered.

Tacama cocked his head, saying in a mocking tone, "What? I can't hear you; say it a bit louder will you? I think my friends and family would like to hear you as well."

Acalan swallowed sharply and looked Tacama dead in the eyes. "*Long live the king!*" He yelled exhaustedly.

Tacama accepted it. "Very good, very good indeed. Yes, long live the king." He looked back at Astrid proudly, grinning widely. She tried her best to hide her fear and so she smiled sweetly.

He said to her happily, "And long live the Azera, right?" Astrid nodded and Tacama turned his attention back to the assassin.

"And with that being said, I think you should be the first benefactor of a kindly king, run before my generosity diminishes."

Wasting no time, Acalan sheathed his swords and took off quickly into the woods. After a while, the sound of heavy footsteps upon the leaves began to fade away.

*f*reedom
*7*ake flight upon our
wings and fly

Shortly after the assassin ran away, Xoco ran up to her son and clutched onto him as if her life depended on it. "Oh dear gods!" She sobbed into his shoulder. "You're safe, my baby is safe!"

Astrid felt like she was able to breathe easy again. She looked down at her shaking hands and crossed them over her chest in an effort to hide her anxiety.

"She's crying," Tepin said, gripping onto the shoulders of both Hitomi and Astrid. "I suppose she has reason to. It's good to know that Tacama is alive and safe and Moha is finally…" She paused, finding it difficult to say *the* word.

Astrid couldn't help but feel that something was wrong. She knew that she should be happy, ecstatic almost. But something wasn't sitting right with her. The same thought kept circling her mind over and over. Even though Moha was a violent man who needed to be stopped, he was still a person.

"Dead." Hitomi said flatly with no emotion in her voice. The other two were a bit surprised to hear Hitomi say it with such ease, especially Astrid. Hitomi couldn't understand why Moha's death bothered them so much.

"He's dead. None of you should be upset about it, this is a good thing."

But he was still a human being, Astrid thought to herself. *He was killed by his own brother. Xoco has just lost a son.*

I know peace wouldn't have been restored until Moha died, but... he was still a man...

Astrid couldn't understand why she was feeling like this. She abhorred the man, she wanted to end his barbarity and to end the killing of the innocent. But she wasn't mentally prepared for the fact that Tacama had killed his own brother. Astrid felt at war with herself.

Still lost in her thoughts, Astrid didn't realize what was happening around her. Tacama was hugging Tepin and asking Hitomi if she was alright and unharmed. Xoco was simply smiling at his son, trying her best to hold back her tears as she stood next to Hitomi with her arm around her. Tacama noticed that Astrid was standing away from the group. Concerned that she was injured, he walked over to her.

Astrid looked up and was caught by surprise as she saw Tacama approach. She felt that she couldn't look at him but she couldn't just look away and pretend that she hadn't seen him coming. She was glad that he was alive of course, but she was afraid that something had changed in Tacama. It was as if he wasn't the same person anymore. His gentle persona had suddenly vanished. This wasn't the same man that she had met within the pyramid.

He appeared to have that gentle look in his eyes. Maybe he hasn't changed at all.

"Astrid! I am happy to see that you are not injured. I have to admit that what you did there, standing up to an assassin, that was courageous. But it was also incredibly stupid." Tacama barked at her, crossing his arms and giving her a stern glare. Astrid felt like she was shrinking in size from fear. That gentle look had instantly vanished. It felt like she was being scolded by the elder priest. She was taken aback by his sudden authority over her.

Trying to think of something to say quickly, she simply mumbled to Tacama, "Sorry." Tacama cocked his head to the side, a confused expression appeared on his face. He reached forward and placed his palm onto her forehead. Astrid jumped at feeling his large hand on her skin. It almost covered her face.

"Hmm... no fever."

Astrid took a step back from him. "W-what?" She whispered.

"Well, less than ten minutes ago you were fighting one of the greatest assassins Moha had to offer, but now you're acting like a shy mouse. Did something happen to you? Did I miss something?" Tacama said. He looked back to the others for an answer but the only reply they gave was an equally confused shrug.

"Fine," Tacama said at last. "Don't tell me what's bothering you. But you will soon. I swear to the gods you'll tell me what this is all about. For now, we have more important things to discuss." He looked at Xoco and said, "Like where your brother is and why you're all in the forest instead of meeting at the rendezvous point, like we planned!"

"You took too long!" Hitomi exclaimed to Tacama and continued, "Cacama went looking for you and he told us to return to the shack. We were heading there when the assassin found us." Tacama growled a curse beneath his breath, unamused with Cacama's interference and with their lack of appreciation.

"Oh, I'm *so sorry.* I didn't mean to keep you waiting, I only had to kill my brother! Now, if you would please listen to me for more than a split second so that I can explain to you every bit of crucial information that I have."

Hitomi scoffed, "I was hoping that'd be the first thing out of your mouth!"

"Will you two stop bickering for a second!" Yelled Tepin, pushing her way between the two of them. They were both surprised at Tepin's sense of authority, she meant business. "We don't have time for this. Just calm down and stop trying to rip each other's head off. Now Tacama, what do we do?"

Tacama muffled a laugh and nodded in approval.

"I think I've managed to convince them that an assassin killed Moha. I'm surprised they believed me since none of them actually knew who I was." Tacama said to the group. They had made it to the shack and they were now huddled together on the floor whilst they waited for Cacama to return.

While they were waiting, Tacama explained the situation to them. "I have told them that I would return once I found you all safely. Astrid, I can return you back to Egypt, my coronation can wait. Just let me know when you are ready. Although, if we do stay here at least another night, it will give me time to gain the trust of the people within the castle. Also, Hitomi, you have the choice of going to Egypt with Astrid. But if you don't want to go, then you are more than welcome to come and live within the palace. You won't have to hide anymore. But I'll leave it up to you to decide. I'll also need some time to find a way to Egypt through the pyramid. I need to make sure that it is the correct gate, one mistake and the destination could be off."

Astrid tucked her knees up to her chest and nodded, looking at the others for some sort of response.

"I think we should stay for one more night" said Tepin. "You're right Tacama, it would give you enough time. The trip is harsh, I remember your father taking me on that boat and it should be as stress free as possible."

Tacama rubbed his knuckles over the stubble of his jaw and sighed, "Alright, then we'll stay." He looked to Xoco who was sleeping beside him, exhausted from their long day. "I'm sure she won't mind, we'll leave for the palace within the hour. Astrid, Hitomi, this will give you two enough time to pack."

Tepin decided to go ahead, taking a still very sleepy Xoco with her. The girls and Tacama were left in the shack. Hitomi seemed to be in a rush, although she hadn't made up her mind about where to go but she seemed to be in a hurry to get somewhere. Astrid however remained silent, still slow in pace while she gathered a blanket and Nefert in her arms.

Tacama helped Hitomi with the small bags she chose to bring - clothes, old belongings from home and a few daggers. She lifted up some of the floorboards and placed her sword beneath them.

"This was here when I first came to this island. I don't know where I'll be going but it should be here for the next person too." She said in a low tone, covering the floor with a rug.

After a few more minutes, Astrid and Hitomi decided that they were ready and the three of them left the shack for the last time.

Since the day she escaped from Moha, Astrid hadn't been able to see the night sky of this realm. Looking up at the starry sky, Astrid had forgotten how beautiful the stars were at midnight. They were glowing above her like a beacon, greeting her warmly. It had been a while since she could sit back and appreciate the beauty of nature. Even though Astrid felt peaceful and relaxed, she couldn't help but think about the choice that Hitomi was yet to make, whether she would choose to come to Egypt with Astrid or stay here.

I wonder what she will do...

Rising from the Ashes

The castle of Tolico was as beautiful as the palace back home. Astrid was now able to see the full majesty of the place. She had a room to herself. The walls were decorated in vibrant colors, forming intricate patterns that were unknown to Astrid. But she still gazed upon them in amazement.

Somehow, she felt like she was home. So much had happened in such short time, it was hard for them all to believe that Tacama's coronation would happen tomorrow, that he had overthrown Moha and would now restore the country to its former glory. Hopefully, things would go smoothly from here on.

The coronation was set to take place at sun rise. Whilst everyone else was sleeping peacefully, Astrid remained wide awake. She knew she should have been sleeping but something kept her awake and alert. Her fingers clutched the edge of the blanket and she stared up at the ceiling, which was decorated in vibrant colors, each pattern becoming intertwined with the next. She was still in shock and her brain couldn't comprehend what had already happened. She was so confused and she had so many questions to ask. But the one person who had the answers she sought was the last person she wanted to see. Just trying to look at him made her entire body tremble with fear.

But why? Another question that played on her mind. She sighed and pulled her knees up to her chest. She hated it when she wasn't able to make sense of things. She rolled onto her side and buried her face deep into her pillow. Her mind was now plagued with so many questions; she knew that she wouldn't be getting any sleep tonight.

In dwelling on her thoughts, she was suddenly interrupted by a loud knock on the door.

"Astrid? It's Tacama. Are you awake?" His voice sounded muffled from the other side, probably trying to speak without anyone noticing.

She was happy but afraid at hearing his voice, perturbed from his previous behavior. Even though she found herself unsettled, she found herself calling out to him. "Yes, come in."

The door creaked open and Tacama stepped inside. He wore a silk tunic that left his arms and the bottom half of his legs exposed. But Astrid immediately thought back to his bloodied clothes and how his demeanor had changed into something unnatural. But he looked quite calm as he stood before her, so perhaps she could look him in the eyes and try to speak to him. But she couldn't help but feel a little uncertain, clinging onto her blanket ever so slightly.

"You know, I said earlier that I was going to talk to you, so here I am." He chuckled, crossing his arms. Despite the gentle laughter, he still remained stern when he looked at Astrid, trying to retain a composed manner. "So, can you tell me why you've been so quiet? It isn't what I said to you about the assassin is it?"

He sighed and sat down beside her. She flinched ever so slightly but he didn't seem to notice.

"Listen to me, what you did back there was truly brave. I'm proud that you stood up against a man who was twice your size. But you could have gotten yourself killed."

"There's always the risk of death in situations like this. I knew that I might die but it didn't matter, I had to do something." Astrid said in a stern tone, trying to make Tacama understand. She lay on her back and stretched her legs out behind Tacama. She stared at the ceiling as she felt exposed when she looked at him, as if he knew what she was thinking by simply looking at her eyes. She wondered why Tacama was doubting her judgment.

"That's a good point." Tacama said gently as he looked up at the ceiling. He seemed to be lost in thought as he gazed at the intricate decoration. He then continued to speak to Astrid in a low tone, "But you need to realize that your actions can be quite rash as they place you and everyone else in danger."

"Did you kill him?" Astrid interrupted. She knew that she should have waited for the right moment but she just couldn't. All she could think about was what Tacama had done and she wanted answers. These questions were making her feel insane.

Tacama was taken aback by Astrid's forwardness; he didn't know how to react. He was shocked at how Astrid could ask such a question. He looked down at the floor and sunk his head into his palms, sighing heavily at the past.

"Yes." He said at last in a gruff voice. "Yes I did." He turned and looked at Astrid with a sombre expression. "Is that why you've been so quiet?... Because you feel that I've become a heartless murderer?"

Astrid sat up abruptly and remained silent for a while, thinking about why she felt this way.

"I knew what the plan entailed," she muttered as she stared at the walls. "I just didn't know that I'd feel like this after it happened. It was a success, you did it. The people of Tolico are free thanks to you, but I..." Astrid lay back down, feeling lost and almost speechless. "I have so many questions and I'm so confused about so many things. Everything is happening so fast and I don't know what to do. I guess I tried to fight Acalan because I didn't know what else to do. I was reckless and stupid and I'm sorry." She sputtered out as she covered her face with her arms, not wanting Tacama to see her face.

"Someone once told me that, 'Stupidity and bravery are the same things from different points of view'." Astrid perked up as she heard him recite her words. She felt embarrassed, feeling that it was a silly thing to say.

Tacama simply smiled and continued, "I think what you did was very brave. I know how you must be feeling though; I've felt that way many times before. It's a terrible feeling, like a heavy burden weighing you down. If something is bothering you, I can help. If you have any questions, I can try to answer them and make you feel more at ease."

Astrid shrugged, saying in a low tone, "I don't really know. I felt like you could answer any question I could ever ask, but now I'm not so sure."

"Well, I could try to answer as many as I can."

Astrid tried to think of a good question but she assumed that none of the questions running through her mind were good enough. So she asked the first question that had been bothering her the most.

"Did Moha have to die? Was there any other option? But I suppose I already know the answer to that one but…"

"Moha was always a determined person who stuck firmly to his opinion." Tacama sighed. "I knew that once his mind had become so twisted and cruel, there was no changing it. The only way to stop his madness was to stop him entirely. I wish that I could've somehow changed him but he was too far gone. Killing him was the only option I had left. What's the next question?" Tacama now looked prepared to answer any question that Astrid had.

"Why did Moha kidnap people with blue eyes?"

"I'll tell you what I know. He thought that people like you and me possessed some sort of supernatural ability, an almost Godlike quality. He believed the power lay in their eyes and he wanted to become more powerful than any other man. So he kidnapped innocent people, killed them and…" Tacama paused for a moment, finding it difficult to finish his sentence.

He swallowed down hard and continued, "He ate them, parts of them. He focused on their hearts or their eyes. He thought that he could somehow absorb their ability that way. The elders believed in eating their enemy as a sign of victory, but they never spoke of absorbing their abilities. For all I know, Moha went mad from his theory and could never return."

Astrid thought back to what had happened between herself and Cacama. How she had made the dagger stop in mid-air. Was this one of the supernatural abilities that Tacama was speaking of?

She sat up once more and took in a deep breath, doing her best to stay calm in asking the next question. She asked Tacama, "What sort of abilities did he think people like us possessed exactly?"

Tacama shrugged and said, "I have no idea, godlike I suppose. The ability to manipulate water, air or fire perhaps. I don't know."

Astrid suddenly realized something. Before this moment, she never really noticed any resemblance between Tacama and his mother, but she finally saw something. Both Xoco and Tacama were extremely bad at lying, their eyes gave it away. Astrid had a feeling that Tacama knew much more than he was saying, but he wouldn't reveal what he knew. So, she decided to feed Tacama information of her own, seeing if he would provide something in return.

"What about a way to stop things from moving?" She suggested.

He looked at her, his face looking confused. He asked in a curious tone, "Could you give me more of an example?"

"A dagger being thrown at you and suddenly stopping in mid-air, right in front of you?" Astrid said shortly, trying to look innocent in her inquiry.

Tacama's expression began to change and she had

the feeling that he was getting the point. He stared at her with a very curious look. "Is this example from personal experience?" He asked in a low tone.

Astrid raised her brows and said teasingly, "Maybe."

He rubbed his fingers over his cleanly shaven jaw and nodded slightly. He grinned as he began to connect the dots.

"You know, when I went to Cacama's house I found one of his most favored daggers dug into the floorboards. Could this also have something to do with this example of yours?" Astrid mimicked his shrug and slyly grinned.

"If blue eyed people are supposed to have these 'god-like abilities', is there a chance that the magic trick you did with the torches back at the pyramid was more than just an illusion?"

Tacama covered his mouth in an attempt to hide his smile. He laughed under his breath and rolled his eyes, Astrid couldn't tell if Tacama was angry or proud at her deduction.

"You've changed a lot since I first met you Astrid," he chuckled. "You're very clever. But your skills of observation may come at a price if you're not careful. I'll let you in on a secret. My brother may have been insane but he didn't get those ideas from thin air, he got them from my father, at least a few of them. Trust me, they were far more than theories. What you saw in the pyramid wasn't a mere illusion. Just like you, I too have discovered the abilities we possess. But by ourselves, we wouldn't know how to control our abilities. That's why the Azera was created in the first place.

There was once a time when the Azera were known in many realms as the teachers who assisted people like us. I don't know if these special abilities make us Godlike but I do know that your spectacle with the knife isn't the end of it. It is only the beginning; this ability you're experiencing can be a great asset to you. But you need to decide on whether or not you want to train yourself in order to control your abilities. I can only make suggestions."

Astrid nodded, brushing her hand through her hair. Even though she felt more assured about Tacama, new questions began to fill her mind. And it was a lot for her to take in, to learn that she has mystical powers that can be used at any time. She needed to decide what to do next.

"Astrid?"

She snapped herself out of her thoughts, realizing that she had been quiet for a little too long. "I was just thinking," she said as she looked at Tacama, "about what you said, for some reason, I'm not finding it that hard to believe. I suppose I could say that these ideas of yours are like stepping into an entirely different realm but I've already done that. You're right though, I have changed for the better. I'm not the same little girl from Egypt."

She looked up at him with a giant smile on her face. "And it's all thanks to you Tacama. No matter how many times I told myself, I thought that I was going to spend the rest of my life like Hitomi, trapped inside that damn shack for the rest of my life. You gave me hope, you gave everyone hope. You told me that your father helped people who were too vulnerable and weak to defend themselves. I realized that I wanted to do something useful with my life. I want to help others and I can do it with my new ability. In confronting Cacama, he was worried about you, thinking that you'd been killed. He doubted our plans and thought we were fighting a hopeless war. I guess you proved him wrong in the end."

Tacama laughed under his breath and clamped a hand on Astrid's shoulder, almost rocking her off balance.

"Like I said, the difference between bravery and stupidity is simply a point of view."

Astrid chuckled, nodding in agreement. She may not have known Tacama very well but she could tell that he was glowing with pride.

Astrid slept soundly for the first time in a long while. But her peaceful slumber didn't last long. A servant had woken her, but Astrid noticed that the moon was still shining brightly. Looking confused, the servant reassured her that the sun would soon be rising. As the sun rose from its slumber, Tolico was ready for the coronation day. Feeling lethargic with sleep, Astrid slowly got ready for the coronation, with a lot of help from the servant. After Astrid had managed to make herself presentable, the servant escorted her towards the ceremony. She was soon met by Hitomi, and Xoco and at first she didn't recognize them as they had been washed and were dressed in vibrant robes.

She looked around the main hall, wondering if this was the same place in which she was almost sacrificed. It was still beautiful to look at, the walls possessed intricate carvings adorned with vivid colors. Astrid, Hitomi and Xoco were escorted to the front of the crowd, concealed by the guards and royal servants who were ordered by Tacama to stay by their side. She had noticed that Tepin had already been seated and she had also noticed them.

Tepin smiled gently and continued to look forward towards the platform. They sat in their seats and were now waiting for the arrival of the new king. Astrid noticed that Tepin had something concealed within a silk sheet. Rather than prying into the mysterious object, she left it alone and looked toward the stage.

The area was filled with curiosity and hushed voices, people wondering who the new king was and what happened to their old king. Some sounded relieved in hearing that the island would have a new king, others remained dubious about whether or not the new one would be just as bad or worse. A few people spoke of Tacama, speculating on the notion of him becoming King. Even Hitomi and Xoco were filled with excitement about the coronation, talking to each other eagerly about what will happen next.

But Astrid remained silent. Her silence was partly due to her fatigue but her mind was elsewhere as the same thought kept repeating itself over and over inside her mind. This was a revelation for Tolico and it was a revelation for herself as she would finally be able to go home to Egypt.

Her thoughts were interrupted by a hushed voice which was coming from a set of opulent burgundy curtains. She assumed it was the Grand Priest preparing for the ceremony.

Xoco tapped Astrid's shoulder and leaned towards her, "It's going to begin soon, try to wake up," she whispered. Astrid gave a tired nod and looked up at the platform in front of her. In front of the crimson curtains was a beautiful golden throne, awaiting its new owner to take his place. The curtains began to move slowly, as if the wind had swept through them. Astrid knew that it was almost time and she wasn't the only one who knew, everyone within the crowd had become silent. The silence was soon broken by the gentle song of flutes from behind the curtains.

As the curtains were slowly drawn away, the coronation began. A man made his way across the stage and stood in front of the throne. He wore a large breastplate that was embellished with ruby and sapphire gems. Instead of the customary white kilt, he wore a multi-colored version which clearly illustrated his importance.

But who was this man? As she squinted at the mystery man, Astrid swore under her breath as she realized who the man was. Tacama. Gods he looked different! His hair had been combed back and he had been washed, thoroughly losing a good layer of dirt and dust. You wouldn't even know that he had spent the last fourteen years stuck within a pyramid. A completely different person now stood before Astrid and the people of Tolico.

Behind Tacama came a priest, carrying, on a thick sheet

of soft fabric, a crown that mimicked Tacama's breastplate. Astrid noticed something distinctive about the crown, something familiar. In the center, surrounded by four red gems was a lapis stone. She glanced down at her chest where the lapis pendant lay and she soon realized that they were both the same stone. Was it intentional or just a coincidence? She looked back up and stared at Tacama's crown, wondering if he had any more secrets. She clutched her pendant tightly and began to shift in her seat.

She was suddenly interrupted by Tepin from behind.

"Girls, just to let you know that this should be like any other coronation. This priest is going to speak in a native tongue so you two probably won't understand. Do you want me to translate for you?" Without thinking, Astrid nodded.

She felt that priest's words wouldn't make any difference to her but she didn't want to refuse Tepin's gesture. He was going to be repeating what hundreds of priests before him have said. He wasn't going to explain what Tacama did to become king or what he did for Tolico as a whole. No one would know, so why did it matter what a priest said during a coronation? *Gods that sounds childish*, Astrid shook herself out of her thoughts.

The priest sputtered out a loud short word and Tacama sat in the throne.

"What did he say?" Hitomi asked.

Tepin adjusted herself so both girls could hear her and she whispered, "Basically, he told Tacama to sit down. Well, he literally said 'let the prince sit' but it's the same thing."

The coronation itself consisted of the priest yelling out odd words that sounded more like coughing than anything else, but Tepin continued to translate.

"Let the prince rise from this throne as a king. Let him take this kingdom into his hands and breath into it a new life." The priest lifted the crown, letting the sheet fall from sight and he raised it above Tacama's head.

"Now let us pray to our king!"

Everyone bowed their heads and Astrid hesitantly followed. She was slightly surprised to see how Hitomi bowed without hesitation. She didn't pray though; the gods already knew what was going on and they knew what Tacama and the others had done. They were watching him closely and required no prayers from Tacama.

She looked up slightly, just enough to still see the stage. The crown was slowly descending towards Tacama's head. Astrid had a feeling that he was going to be crowned whilst everyone had their heads turned down. Hitomi wouldn't want to miss this so Astrid ever so slightly prodded her friend's hand. Hitomi tilted her head slightly towards Astrid.

"Look" she whispered.

The girls both looked up at Tacama just as the glimmering crown was placed upon his head. That's when Hitomi did something a little out of character.

She reached over, grabbed Astrid's hand and leaned over to her, whispering into her ear, "We did it Astrid, we did it."

Astrid gripped Hitomi's hand and laughed under her breath. She rested her head against Hitomi's and whispered in return, "That we did."

The priest spoke once more and after a moment, Tepin translated again. "Raise your heads and let our king speak."

Tacama stood and smiled proudly at the crowd. "Thank you Grand Priest," he said, respectfully bowing his head towards the priest beside him.

Tacama let out a big breath and turned back towards his people, "Many things have happened within the last few weeks," he said in a loud clear voice that was filled with strength, "including the death of my brother, our former King Moha. But fear not my people, I promise you that Tolico will be reborn. Every single soul within this kingdom is *safe* from any danger that lurks outside of our country. As king, I will do everything in my power to protect you all. But I must admit that I could not do this alone. Tolico would not be as protected as it is now without the help of two young women from another land. Many of you may remember my father King Necalli. He traveled to distant realms to protect and defend people who were vulnerable and weak. You will all be pleased to know that my father's soul lives on within the souls of two young women." Tacama looked over to Astrid and Hitomi and stretched his hands out towards them. "And if they will join me upon this stage, I will reward them for such courage and strength."

Wait, what? Astrid thought. *Rewarding me? For courage?* She couldn't comprehend what was happening; it was hard for her to swallow. But it seemed that Hitomi was more than eager to accept her reward. She gripped Astrid's hand tighter and stood up, practically dragging Astrid along with her.

Everything seemed to blur past her but Astrid kept her head forward as they both made their way toward Tacama. Climbing up a small set of stairs, they both stood next to the King of Tolico.

Tacama's smile grew and he placed a hand on Astrid's shoulder. "This is Astrid and Hitomi," he said to the crowd, "One, a princess from the land called Egypt, the other from Japan. These girls do not belong to Tolico, they never have, but they stood by my side to protect a kingdom that wasn't theirs. Very few are brave enough to defend strangers and I am confident when I say that these women have the courage of a god." He nodded towards the crowd once more and another woman stood up from the front row.

Tepin? She made her way to the stage with a silken sheet of her own in her hands, carrying two bronze circlets that were decorated with lapis and golden flowers. Tepin had a sly grin upon her face, obviously happy with the fact that Hitomi and Astrid never saw this coming. She stood on the other side of Tacama and held out the sheet.

Tacama began to speak once more, "One of these crowns was made for my mother, Queen Xoco and when my younger sister Izel had her own coronation, a duplicate was created. These crowns no longer have an owner, they have no meaning in this realm, so I shall give them new ones. Made with the strongest brass and the most beautiful of lapis, these crowns symbolize great courage and beauty. These princesses before us possess both of these qualities. Even when they return to their kingdom, these crowns will always remind them of their great deeds here in Tolico." He turned away from the girls, carefully taking one of the circlets and he returned to them, this time he was facing Hitomi.

"So, let us all bless Princess Hitomi of Japan and thank her for her bravery. From now on, our countries will have a bond like no other as we will defend our people to the death."

The crowd erupted into applause, none of which were outmatched by Xoco who was bawling in the front row. Tacama placed the circlet upon Hitomi and kissed the top of her head. "Thank you." He whispered.

Tepin walked over to her cousin and Tacama took the other circlet from the sheet. "And let us bless Princess Astrid of Egypt and thank her for her bravery. Without these women, Tolico would be left in the dark." Tacama could obviously see how shocked Astrid was. He laughed and placed the crown upon her wavy black hair and kissed the top of her head as he did with Hitomi. "Thank you Astrid," he said patting her shoulders, "and stop acting so surprised. You deserve this. You said you wanted to be like my father, well little do you know that you already are."

One Step Closer

Astrid sat on a bench in one of the many libraries within the Tolico palace. She looked up at the numerous scrolls, wondering how many there were and if someone had been able to read them all. Some, covered in dust and cobwebs, looked older than others. They had been waiting for Tacama to return so that he could inform them of their departure to Egypt. Until then, Tepin, Hitomi and Xoco seemed to be caught in a conversation of their own, most likely to keep their worried thoughts at bay. Astrid however was not too interested in their discussion. She had learned that sometimes it is better to get caught up in your own thoughts. Besides, she wasn't one for conversation filled with small talk.

Astrid rested her head in her palm while inspecting her new circlet. She didn't know if it was strange that she felt odd when wearing it. Hitomi looked proud to have her own atop her head. Ever since the coronation she hadn't taken it off. Astrid had the feeling that Hitomi liked wearing it because it made her feel special. She was no longer a forgotten princess left to live the rest of her life in a rotting shack out in the forest. Astrid wondered if she was going to stay in Tolico. Hitomi would be respected as the hero she was if she stayed. In Egypt, both girls would probably have to keep every moment of their experience a total secret. Hitomi may have been offered to stay with Astrid, but was that really the best for her?

Before she could dwell on the subject, the doors beside her swung open and King Tacama stepped inside. He was no longer dressed in his flamboyant attire, he looked more himself with his hair messy, wearing a simple kilt and a cheeky grin. He didn't look much like a king in this attire, but no one cared. It felt like everyone was more comfortable in seeing Tacama casual and acting like his old self again. But what mattered most of all to Astrid was that no matter what fancy robes he wore, he was her friend.

"So!" Tacama said, his voice booming, "Astrid, I think it's about time for you to go home."

Astrid's heart felt like it could have leapt out of her chest. "Seriously?" She stuttered. "We get to leave now?"

Tacama nodded with a smile, "In a few minutes, yes. I have told everyone within the palace about both of your situations but I only told them what they needed to hear. I have told the guards and the servants that an assassin had kidnapped both of you some time ago; I eliminated the culprit and I needed to bring both of you back to your homes. Hitomi, if you do choose to stay here, I have also informed them that you may not have a home to return to. Trust me, I didn't say too much, just the necessary details. We'll be leaving within the hour so make sure you've packed your belongings. Meet me back here the moment you're all done."

Astrid was delighted to have confirmation that she would be going home and soon but she felt for Hitomi who had a difficult decision to make.

Tacama continued, "We should leave the palace without being seen. That henchman of Moha's is still alive and despite his cowardice, I am certain that his stupidity may yet lead to confrontation. He may track us down for all we know. We'll leave the palace when everything has quietened down and we can get back to the Tolico Pyramid. With luck, everything should work out well."

Everyone had their belongings packed and were ready

to leave as they met back in the library. As silent as a mouse, Tacama led the group out of the palace and into the forest.

"As I said before, nobody knows where we are or where we are going." Said Tacama, carefully making his way through the dense brush while clearing a path for the others to follow. "The only person who would have any idea of where we are is Cacama. Mother, have you heard from him yet?" Xoco shook her head, sniffling from the cold of the night air.

"No, but I assume he has put himself in hiding. Cacama may not have agreed with Moha's actions but he was still close to him. I wouldn't be surprised if he went back to my home, panicked and hid. He did the same thing when our family…" she paused, swallowing hard and looking back at Astrid and Hitomi. They both smiled gently and Astrid held her hand.

Tepin stopped in her tracks, she went up onto her toes and wrapped her arms around her cousin's shoulders.

"You, your royal majesty, need to stop worrying. We have more important things to be concerned about, like getting these two safely home. We know what my father does, he panics. He always has and always will. Let him have his temper tantrum in peace and we can deal with it when we return." She let go of Tacama and spun around on her heels, a cheeky grin spread across her face, "Isn't that right you two?" She asked them both.

Hitomi grabbed tightly onto her belongings and nodded, answering for both her and for Astrid. Astrid was still shaken up from the last few hours and all that had passed and was now thinking about what was yet to come. She still couldn't get over the fact that she was finally leaving this place. However, she still didn't know what was going to happen once she got to Egypt. Would she ever see these four again?

Tepin's giant yet honestly adorable smile, Xoco's kind,

honest words and Tacama's wisdom. And Hitomi, what would happen to her? Would she come and stay with Astrid or live in Tolico? Or, the most unlikely of choices, return to Japan, her home. Would Astrid ever see Hitomi's dirty looks again? She knew it was odd but it was the small things that mattered the most to Astrid and she knew that she would miss them all.

Tacama led the girls across the river, using the rotting remains of a bridge. This would have made it easier for Hitomi and Astrid to see the pyramid from this bridge, but it was a shame the structure – or what remained of it – was too far from Hitomi's shack.

With only a sliver of the moon's silver rays to guide the group to the pyramid, Astrid was surprised that any of them could see where they were going. She couldn't see anything past Tepin's stark white dress. But she kept walking, concentrating hard on Tepin and making sure that Hitomi was still holding on to the back of her cloak. Astrid assumed that Hitomi couldn't see much either, but gods did she have to have such a tight hold onto the waist of Astrid's cloak? It felt like at any moment the fabric may rip from underneath Hitomi's stubby fingernails.

She wondered if Hitomi was afraid of the dark. What a funny thought, a strong girl like Hitomi couldn't have such a simple fear… right? Astrid shouldn't ask, it was clear – from each and every one of them – that they were all afraid, even if they didn't make it obvious.

For all she knew, Hitomi wasn't afraid of the dark, she was more afraid of what lay ahead. She hoped that soon, Hitomi wouldn't have to worry, that no one would have to be fearful. She hadn't realized until then how much everyone had sacrificed for this so called 'rebellion'. At least it was coming to an end.

Finally they made it to the pyramid. The large barrier of brush and wild plants had somehow managed to reconstruct itself, hiding the beauty behind it. Once again there didn't appear to be a door and Astrid wondered how they would get to the other side.

"Everyone stand back." Said Tacama loudly, putting his arm out to keep the girls from coming any farther. "Stay back and turn your heads away."

Turn your heads? Astrid thought. *But why? What did Tacama not want us to see?* One after the other, they all turned their heads, all seeming to understand why but Astrid stood there, still wondering why the whole act was necessary.

Everyone, including Tacama, had assumed that Astrid would turn her head. Before she knew what was happening the barrier burst into flames. Tacama looked behind him and winked at Astrid.

"Magic tricks, right?" He whispered.

A smile spread across her face. *So that's why he wanted everyone to turn their heads.* No one knew about Tacama's 'magic tricks', perhaps Xoco was kept in the dark as well.

"You can all look now. Everyone, if you'll follow me." Tacama called out, walking over a pile of ashes once belonging to a strip of the barrier. Astrid followed close by and Hitomi gripped onto Astrid's hand, slightly terrified about how the barrier had become a pile of ash.

"Astrid, Hitomi." Tacama called out as he led them through the pyramid. "The pyramid, as I've said before, protects and controls a river. Tepin and my mother have seen this plenty of times when I was a child but I'm sure that you two will be very much confused when you see the gates for the first time. The river is more of an ocean and with a sturdy vessel, you can sail to any realm you could ever imagine. I remember the first time I traveled on the river. It's a beast, that's for sure and it'll leave you feeling awful but that will pass. I'm not sure whether this water has anything to do with any other river but by the gods it'll beat you raw the first few times!"

They couldn't tell if he was just joking or if he was being serious. He clamped a hand onto Tepin's shoulder and began to laugh. "The first time you traveled this way you looked like you had just eaten the organs of a rotting pig, you poor thing. But then again, you are a bit of a wimp."

Tepin scoffed and rolled her eyes, shoving her cousin hard in the side before turning around. "Don't listen to him," she growled. "He's just trying to sound like he was great on his first time! He was sicker than a stray dog! You'll do fine though, as long as you don't stuff your faces the whole time!"

Despite the two of them play fighting, Astrid didn't find it all too funny. She'd rather not feel ill but then again she didn't really care, she just wanted to go home. After everything she has been through, she wasn't going to let a scary river stop her from getting back to her family.

The group continued to push on. She didn't remember the hallway being this long when she was here last time. Even though Hitomi and Astrid had come before, it felt like it had gotten a lot bigger since then. The pyramid didn't look this big from the outside. It was tiny when compared to most pyramids she had seen in Egypt but gods it didn't seem that way on the inside.

The River

As the group continued to walk along the hallway, something at the end began to shimmer brightly. This immediately caught everyone's attention and Astrid and Hitomi started to run towards the mysterious glow. It was shining brightly like a beacon, luring the group in like a bunch of moths to a flame. As they got closer, they came to an abrupt halt as they couldn't go any further.

Blocking their path was a wall filled with rows of golden and crimson blocks, all of them identical in shape and size. They had never seen anything like this before, it was like another mural from the palace, except this one was designed with precision and what appeared to be a calculated pattern. They were soon met by the others and Tacama marched towards the glittering wall. He began to inspect each brick, gliding his fingers gently across their surface.

"Astrid, come here." Tacama called out. "I'm going to need your help for a moment." Astrid nodded and ran up beside him. Upon closer inspection, she noticed that each brick possessed a unique pattern that had been engraved within the surface.

Amazing. Astrid thought to herself. Some of the patterns were rectangular and others consisted of spirals and stars, each pattern being very unique and intricate. But Astrid noticed that these patterns were resting within a larger, very familiar shape. It was a teardrop that had been carved within the surface while the pattern rested within the concave of the teardrop. It looked like the bricks were waiting for something to take place within each drop. Tacama picked off the dust from one of the center stones and held his hand out toward Astrid.

"Your pendant, it's the key to Egypt's gate. I had sent that cat after you in the hope that you would find the key and somehow find your way here. Hitomi, your gate is a little bit harder to come across as I had no idea where you came from so I was unable to help you. But do not fret, we will get you home." Astrid slipped her necklace over her head and handed it to Tacama. Hopefully, everyone would be home soon.

Tacama took the necklace by the pendant and slipped the stone's face into the rock. "Step back now." He said and with a loud rumble, the wall began to separate from its center.

As the bricks parted, a maroon door emerged and replaced the glimmering wall as it pushed itself forward. In the center of the door lay a row of shimmering gold blocks, instantly catching Astrid's attention. As she looked closer, she saw that inscribed on the blocks were Egyptian hieroglyphics. The sight of the hieroglyphics filled Astrid with intense joy whereas everyone else looked upon them with both confusion and wonder.

"Whoa, what is that Tacama?" Tepin asked, scooting her way towards her cousin and Astrid. "I've never seen letters like that before."

For once, Astrid could do the translating. The letters alone made her feel one step closer to home. With pride, she said aloud to the others, "It reads Luxor, Egypt," she grinned as she looked over at Tepin, "it's the written language of Egypt, my home."

Hitomi clamped a hand on Astrid's shoulder. "Thank gods, for once we don't have to read it for you!" She said in a cheerful tone.

Tacama chuckled and said, "That's right. From now on

Astrid, you'll have to do the translating for all of us. Now, would you do us the honor of opening it?"

Astrid sighed with relief and smiled. She nodded and placed her hand on the door. As she gently pushed at its surface the door opened and she was met by a strong gust of wind that knocked her back.

The humidity of the wind had attacked her face, causing her skin to feel sweaty and agitated. Suddenly, a glowing blue lake erupted from the darkness. Never in her entire life had she ever seen anything as beautiful as this. Xoco gasped in amazement and Hitomi swore aloud at the sight of such an amazing spectacle.

"Now that is something!" Hitomi said in shock.

Xoco hugged both Hitomi and Astrid from behind and said to them in a cheerful tone, "That it is. Gods I haven't seen this in years. It's truly a gift from the heavens."

Tacama nodded in agreement but his expression remained serious as he stared at the surface of the water. Obviously he was ready to leave and they would have plenty of time to admire the river in due course.

He stepped within the doorway and grabbed a long piece of rope from the ground that mysteriously appeared as the light shone on it. It seemed to be attached to something but they couldn't see what. Tacama pulled at it, waiting for something to emerge. Just as a small pile of rope began to pile around his feet, the bow of a boat slowly came into view, gliding across the luminous river. As it got closer, Astrid noticed that there was a slight drop between the doorway and the boat.

"Everyone should be able to fit in just fine. There are larger boats but this one should be more than adequate for our needs." Tacama said. He wrapped the rope tightly around his hand, testing to make sure that it was firm and sturdy. He then turned towards the group and asked, "Can one of you grab a torch from behind you? It'll be bright enough when we get inside but we'll need some light in order to see the boat better, unless you want to take a swim."

Xoco grabbed the nearest torch and handed it over to her son. Tacama hitched it onto a hook within the doorway and stepped back.

He then looked at Tepin with a sly grin. "Tepin, how about you go in first and show the girls what you're *not* supposed to do."

Tepin scoffed and shoved her way through, slapping her cousin on the back of the head as she headed forward. Barely lit by the flame, Astrid saw Tepin standing on the edge of the doorway. Without any warning, she suddenly jumped into the darkness. Astrid's heart skipped a beat at the sight of Tepin's leap. What if she had missed the landing? But instead of hearing a large splash, she heard the distinct sound of sandals against wood.

"See? I did great!" Tepin called out from the darkness confidently. Astrid could only imagine the smile on Tepin's face in proving that she could do it. "Who's next?" Tepin asked aloud.

Hitomi released Astrid's hand from her grip and, taking a deep breath, she looked up at Tacama. "Are you sure it's safe?" She muttered.

Tacama smiled at her and nodded reassuringly. The look in her eyes revealed the fear she felt about this unavoidable leap of faith. Astrid wondered why Hitomi was afraid of jumping into the boat. After everything they've been through so far, this would be their easiest endeavor.

Perhaps Hitomi cannot swim? Astrid thought to herself. Then again, the thought of being caught in that river would make anyone afraid, regardless of whether or not they could swim.

Tepin stretched out her arm from the darkness and said aloud, "Come on Hitomi, it's going to be fine. I can't swim and I've traveled along this river dozens of times as a child.

I haven't fallen off so far!"

Hitomi looked over at Astrid for some encouragement and Astrid smiled in return, which made Hitomi feel more reassured than before. Astrid gave her a friendly push forward and without further delay, she grabbed hold of her bag and jumped into the darkness and was met by the study base of the boat.

"Are you ready to go next dear?" Xoco asked from behind. She rested a hand on Astrid's shoulder and kissed the back of her head.

Astrid's body shook at the thought of jumping into the black abyss, wondering if she would miss the landing by an inch and be lost in the river. Astrid knew that the more she thought about it, the worse she felt. She also knew that she couldn't stay here for long, people were waiting for her and so was her home. With a deep breath, she ran towards the doorway and into the darkness. The ground beneath her feet vanished as she leapt forward, praying that she would land in the boat.

She had the sense of falling down towards the river, her heart beating rapidly with each second. Suddenly, her feet landed on the base of the boat and to her relief she saw Hitomi and Tepin. She gave out a sigh of relief as she fell onto her bottom, glad that it was over.

"Not as scary as you'd think, is it?" Tepin laughed.

Astrid opened her eyes and nodded, but there was something terrifying about it. As she looked around, she couldn't believe what she saw. Tacama was right, it *was* bright inside here. The water was clear blue and it was constantly glowing, as if the sky had been captured within the river. It was amazing.

Tacama helped Xoco onto the boat. From behind him, he then closed the door and made sure it was locked tight. They were now blocked from the realm of Tolico. He turned around and leapt onto the boat. He took a seat with the others and handed the necklace back to Astrid. This boat was clearly larger than an average boat as everyone had managed to fit in with enough space to spare, but it wasn't nearly as large as a ship. Perhaps it was a unique quality of the pyramid. Everyone's belongings were secure on the boat and everyone was ready for the voyage.

But Tacama appeared to be disheartened, as if their whole venture was depressing by the fact that it was soon to end. But when he realized that Astrid was beginning to notice his demeanor he replaced his expression with an excited grin.

"Ready to go home Astrid?"

Petrichor

After a while, everyone seemed to relax and enjoy the voyage. Tacama was looking back toward the door to Tolico as it became smaller and smaller, slowly fading away from sight. Tepin was sitting beside him, sleeping soundly with her head resting on Xoco's shoulder. Astrid and Hitomi were sprawled out beside one another, their tiny feet hanging over the edge of the boat and Astrid's hair floating in the river's waves, the river's glow illuminating the darkness of her hair. The trip to Egypt would take less than a day and they'd arrive by morning, at least that's what Tacama had said.

An hour into their journey and everyone was completely exhausted. It was as if the last few days had finally caught up with them. Even though Astrid could barely keep her eyes open, she just couldn't sleep. Well, that's what she thought. When she thought she had come to terms with the fact that she wouldn't be getting any sleep, she then fell into a deep slumber. It was as if the gods had pitied her and placed her under a spell of rest. She didn't dream of anything as both her body and mind were too tired to conjure up an images at all. She rested in the emptiness of her mind like a baby in her mother's arms, with the waves gently rocking her.

Out of the depths of her sleep, she heard a very odd sound from the world around her.

Ignore it, she thought. Wait – no. No, she had heard that sound before, it was a splash of water. Gods that seemed loud, it couldn't be a fish, so what is it? *Oh gods, someone's in the river!*

Astrid woke and jumped up in shock. She panted frantically from the sound and looked around the boat. Everyone else seemed to be asleep. Xoco, Tepin, Tacama, Hito - wait... Where was Hitomi?

The waves thrashed around rapidly and amidst the violence of the water Astrid caught a glimpse of Hitomi's head just above the surface before falling under the crashing waves.

"Hitomi!" Astrid screamed out to the river. Everyone woke to the sound of her screams, looking bewildered at Astrid. "She fell off! She's in the river!" Astrid was pointing at the water and her words were drowned out by the sound of the waves. Tacama pushed his way through and stood beside Astrid, looking for Hitomi in the river. Astrid's heart sank as she tightly gripped the side of the boat. The waves were beginning to calm down. Something was wrong, why couldn't they see her? Astrid felt helpless as she sat there and stared at the river in anticipation.

"I have to go after her!" She yelped as she began to pull off her dress.

Tacama quickly grabbed her arm. "You can't do that Astrid! No one knows how deep this river goes! You could get yourself killed!"

Astrid shoved him off and yanked off her clothes, throwing them behind her. "I don't care!" She yelled. "I'm not going to let Hitomi die, not now!" With that, she took a deep breath and jumped off the boat, plunging deep into the luminous river.

The impact of the cold water shocked her entire body, causing her muscles to tense. As soon as she opened her eyes, the sting from the water was almost overwhelming. But she needed to ignore the pain and find Hitomi. She blinked repeatedly until the pain subsided and she could see properly again. She looked forward, the river's glow giving her the perfect lighting to search for Hitomi. She couldn't call out for her and she had no idea where to look. She dove under the surface, scanning the space around her. With how deep it went, it was more like an ocean than a river. Her chest felt tight, not from lack of air but from her own anxiety. She had to find Hitomi; she couldn't let her die here, not after everything they've been through.

She suddenly spotted something in the corner of her eye. At first she thought it may have been a fish, but as she swam closer towards it, she realized that it was *far* too long to be a fish.

Hitomi! It looked like she was unconscious and she was slowly sinking deeper and deeper into the river; her body was far from fighting. Astrid swam quickly forwards towards her friend. Her body was surging with pain and her lungs felt like they were going to burst from the lack of air. They needed to reach the boat quickly. She grabbed Hitomi around the waist and pulled her and upwards toward the boat. Hitomi's body was dragging her down and it was difficult for Astrid to swim with only one arm. The image of the boat was getting smaller. But she wasn't going to give up now, she had to get them both onto that boat.

Tacama, Tepin and Xoco waited anxiously for them to appear from the river. Tacama remained calm and composed whereas the other two were panic-stricken. Xoco suddenly noticed something coming closer to the surface.

"There she is!" Cried Xoco and Astrid emerged from the river with Hitomi still unconscious. She began to pant for air but the waves kept going over them. Xoco leaned over the edge of the boat and reached out for the girl's. Tepin grabbed hold of Xoco's back, worried that she might also fall in. Astrid swam towards them with great difficulty, her body ready to give up at any moment. But with another labored breath and a mighty push, Astrid reached the boat and shoved Hitomi's limp body forward.

She didn't care if she was stuck in the water; Hitomi was the main priority. While Tepin and Xoco rushed to check on Hitomi, Tacama stretched out his hand toward Astrid. He looked a bit angry but mostly surprised at what she had just done. She grabbed his arm and let him pull her up.

She quickly threw on the dry dress which clung to her wet body as she dashed to Hitomi's side.

"Is she alright? Is she breathing?" She barked. "Is she alive?" No one answered her. Tepin and Xoco were in too much shock from the whole event to say anything. Astrid pushed her way between Xoco and Tepin and grabbed Hitomi's limp form.

"Wake up!" She yelled, "Come on, damn it! You're not gonna die now! Not after all this! I won't let you! Wake up Hitomi, come on just breathe." She cried, shaking Hitomi like a rag doll and she struck at Hitomi's chest with immense force. "Wake up!"

Hitomi suddenly coughed, opened her eyes and began to move. A mouthful of water sprouted out and she tried to sit up, but the water was still making its way from her lungs. Everyone simultaneously sighed in relief. Astrid helped Hitomi to sit up and gently patted her back. She wasn't going to let her choke now. Hitomi gagged on the water, vibrant blue drops splattered onto the floor of the boat.

"It's alright, Hitomi. Just breathe, come on, it's alright. You're safe." Astrid said to her in a soft tone, soothing her and helping her sit up, "Just breath."

At last, Hitomi managed to cough up all of the water she had breathed in, she slowly relaxed and took a deep gulp of air. She dropped back against Astrid, totally exhausted. She opened her mouth and tried to speak but nothing came out.

"No, no, just rest dear." Xoco said softly. "There's no need to talk." Hitomi nodded, her eyelids drooping from exhaustion. Astrid let out a heavy and tired sigh, it felt as though everyone around her was fading away and her only focus was Hitomi.

She brushed her hand through Hitomi's damp hair. "You're safe now," she whispered. "Go to sleep and think of something nice. Think about the petrichor; fragrant raindrops hitting the leaves, the soft mud between your toes, the scent of warm rain on stones."

Astrid soon let her eyes rest as well, taking in the smell of the water around her soaked hair and body. Their adventure was coming to an end at last and she now had nothing else to worry about, nothing at all.

After their stressful situation, everyone had managed to fall back to sleep. But rather than sleeping separately, they all slept together in a group, Astrid rested in the center along with Hitomi, checking every so often that she was alright. As the others slept, Astrid lay awake and munched on a piece of corn that Xoco had packed for the trip.

Astrid knew she didn't have to watch over Hitomi like a hawk, she was safe with the others surrounding her, but she couldn't help it. She felt as though this was all her fault. If she had known that Hitomi couldn't swim, she could have somehow prevented her from falling, or maybe she shouldn't have dragged her along to the pyramid to begin with. She just didn't want anyone, especially Hitomi, to get harmed so that she could return home.

"Stop looking so sad, Astrid." Astrid jumped at the sound of the raspy voice and almost dropped her corn. But she looked down to see Hitomi gently smiling back at her, she was now half awake and slowly reaching for Astrid's hand. "It's OK." Hitomi mumbled softly.

Astrid let out a heavy breath. She had been honest with Tacama and trusted him with everything she said; so she could trust Hitomi as well and tell her what was on her mind. After all they have been together for a while.

But as she was about to speak, Hitomi interrupted and said in a hushed tone, "You don't have to say anything, just let me talk, OK? I want to thank you for saving my life. I've been mean to you and I shouldn't have been. I thought you were pathetic and weak but you're not. You're braver than I ever was and it took me a while to realize that. I was too frightened to even leave the forest; I disconnected myself from everybody, even Xoco. I got used to being alone, but when I got to know all of you, it was nice... To have people who looked out for me. I was afraid to lose you all like I did my own family. I know that they died so long ago and I barely remember them. But... I do know that they died because of me and I don't want any other people to sacrifice themselves for me. But you saved my life and you could have gotten yourself killed but you didn't care. We don't even know each other that well and yet you saved me. But I guess that's the kind of person you are."

Astrid was in awe, she had never expected Hitomi to say anything like that.

"I... I don't know what to say," she stuttered in surprise. Hitomi's sincerity had struck Astrid in the heart and she knew she had to say something in return.

"I want you to live with me in Egypt. You deserve a home of your own; to no longer live in fear of what may come. Let me give you that home Hitomi, please. My parents will be able to arrange something in order to let you stay, I know it. You don't have to come if you don't want to, you can go back to Tolico but I don't know if I'll ever see you again. I don't want you to be a memory, I want you to be my friend, my family... if you want."

Hitomi slowly sat up, her eyes glazed over with emotion.

"You won't have to worry about not being able see us again." Tacama, was beside them, clamping a hand on both Hitomi's and Astrid's shoulders. "This is a bridge from Tolico to Egypt, when we get to your home Astrid, I'll show you how to navigate your own pyramid. You'll be able to visit Tolico any time you like and I'll come see you too, we all will. And Hitomi, I think you should stay with Astrid in Egypt, I knew that from the beginning. There's no reason for you to stay in the country that has caused you so much pain. Go live in Egypt, have a new life, a new home, a family of your own. I know you'll be truly happy there. Besides, you deserve to be the princess that you truly are and I believe Egypt will welcome you. Of course you will always be welcome here, but I fear that here, the only thing you could be is a guest of the palace and I don't think that's fair. You deserve so much more than that."

Hitomi looked more nervous than ever. She looked down at her lap, thinking over what they had just said. Astrid reached forward and rested her hand atop of Hitomi's. She wasn't begging for a reply, she only wanted Hitomi to know that she was there for her.

Hitomi jumped forward and engulfed Astrid in a hug. The impact caused them both to fall over and with that the boat rocked. Tacama held onto the edge of the boat with both hands, worried that they would all topple into the river.

"OK!" She cried, "OK, I'll come. I'll come and stay in Egypt. Thank you Astrid." Astrid laughed and the two girls hugged each other more tightly. Astrid had never seen her smile like that before, perhaps Hitomi had never been that happy in all her life.

"Now that that has been resolved, there's something I want to discuss with you two." Tacama said sternly, his smile hidden beneath his stern expression. Both Hitomi and Astrid sat up and gave Tacama their full attention. "Both of our kingdoms are safe now, but we made a promise to each other, that we would stay together, side by side and protect Tolico to the death, remember?" They nodded in unison, waiting to hear what he would say next. "Since we are going our separate ways I suggest we alter our vow. We will now serve as guardians for the weak and vulnerable, we will protect the realms from people like Moha. Are you both willing to do this?"

Astrid smiled gently at Tacama.

"I am more than willing to do this. I told you both that I don't want anyone else to endure such fear and terror at the hands of people like Moha. I will do everything in my power to prevent such cruelty from happening." She smiled proudly and nudged Hitomi, "To the death, right?"

Hitomi smiled and grabbed her hand, "Right, to the death."

Having slept soundly for a couple hours, Astrid was awoken by Tacama gently nudging her shoulder in an attempt to rouse her. With eyes half open, she saw that everyone was eating.

"Astrid, you should get some food." She groaned and rubbed her face vigorously, trying to remove the sleep from her eyes. She really didn't want to wake up, her body felt too relaxed to even move. She wondered why they couldn't just wake her up when they got to Egypt.

Wait, are we already here?! Astrid got up quickly and almost made the boat rock violently from her enthusiasm. She glanced around, hoping to see the golden sand of the Egyptian desert and to be greeted by a warm breeze. But she was only met by the luminous river flowing calmly beneath them.

Astrid simply stared at the water with annoyance while Xoco looked at her and smiled.

"Astrid, don't startle yourself like that," said Xoco, "come and eat, we'll shortly be in Egypt." Astrid let out a heavy sigh and cursed the river for being so long. She then sat down with everyone else and tried to hide her annoyance from the others.

Xoco wrapped a softened piece of flat-bread around

some dried meat and passed it over to Astrid. Her stomach growled with hunger and without wasting another second she took a large bite from the thick flat-bread. Astrid wondered how Xoco was even able to cook on a boat in the middle of a river. There was obviously no source of fire or any sort of heat... wait.

Astrid finally joined the dots. She tried to hide it from the others but she couldn't resist laughing at the thought of Tacama setting fire to a pile of flat-breads. She had almost forgotten about his special abilities, they definitely worked to their advantage, that's for sure. Sometimes she couldn't believe that this was real, it felt like it was something out of a potion-induced dream.

The peace of their meal was suddenly broken by the roars of Tacama's rage as he began to curse from the top of his lungs and slammed his fists against a wall. She turned around to see Tacama kicking a giant stone wall that now blocked their path.

It took Astrid a while to realize that their boat had come to a standstill as a stone wall was now blocking their path. She had been so preoccupied by thoughts of Egypt, on finally getting home, that her mind had distracted her from reality.

Tacama continued to curse at the wall and punched it until his knuckles became sore.

"Damn it! We'd be there by now but I just can't find a way to tie this rope to that damn pole."

"Okay Tacama, how about you take a break." Tepin yelled, "Gods know we don't need to see another one of your childish outbursts again." She sighed and rolled her eyes, suggesting that this wasn't the first time that Tacama has done something like this.

She looked over at Astrid and reassured her, saying, "Just ignore him. The reason he's so angry is because he can't get past the gate. To get past the gate, you need to decode it and he can't decode it if he can't secure the boat long enough."

Astrid took a bite of her food and turned around, watching Tacama being furious over a piece of rope and a stone pole. She wondered if there was any way that she could help him, aside from knocking him out so no one would have to deal with his childish behavior.

"You know what? It's useless! Absolutely useless!" Tacama yelled as he kicked the wall for a final time and threw the rope down. Astrid handed her food over to Hitomi to hold and she walked over to Tacama, picking the rope up from the boat. She looked up at him and smiled.

"Here, let me see if I can help. You go and eat." She said as she sat down at the bow of the boat. He begrudgingly went towards the others and sat down. She looked at the stone pole that was only a few inches from her, trying to figure out the great difficulty in securing it. She twisted the rope between her fingers, inspecting every inch of the stone pole while curling her toes in the cool water below her.

She then realized what Tacama was missing and it was quite clear from her angle. At the base of the wooden bow was a small divot, one that could have easily been overlooked while standing up. She took the rope, quickly looping it through the bow and then looping it over the pole, knotting it tightly.

"Nothing's too hard if you look at it from a different perspective," she laughed as she looked over at Tacama. But she couldn't tell if he wanted to hug her or kill her. Perhaps it was a little of both.

"Yeah thanks. Now go eat," he said in a gruff tone. To prevent any more outbursts, she simply went to the others. But she wondered how he could have overlooked something as simple as that.

The stress of recent events would have tested any man on top of which Tacama has the future of Tolico on his shoulders. But what if there was more... she hoped he wasn't hiding anything from her and the others.

Astrid was so close to Egypt, she could almost taste it. According to Tacama, on the other side of the stone wall was the Egyptian pyramid. But before they could get through, Tacama needed to translate the message that was carved into the wall. Astrid was puzzled as she assumed that she'd be able to recognize the writing but alas she did not, as it wasn't in any form of Egyptian hieroglyphics that she knew.

Every second felt like an hour to Astrid. She knew Tacama was nearly finished translating and that it should only take him a few minutes. But she couldn't help but feel restless whilst everyone else calmly ate. They were all aware that Astrid was frustrated but there was nothing they could do.

Tacama needed to take his time with this and he couldn't afford any mistakes. He had no idea what lurked within this pyramid or how it worked; it might be filled with countless traps that could destroy their vessel.

Astrid knew that Egyptian pyramids had secret traps as she had seen hundreds of spells and warnings showing how complex these could be. For all she knew, the unknown hieroglyphics that Tacama was working to decipher might be a warning.

"Astrid, can I get your help?" Tacama asked as he brushed of a thick layer of dirt from the lower half of the wall. Astrid took one last bite of the flat-bread and then joined him, a newfound worry began to sink into her brain. "The glyphs change right here, I've never seen them before," he muttered. "The language inscribed here usually belongs to the kingdom beyond the wall. So, I was hoping that you'd recognize them." After Tacama brushed away the remaining dirt, Astrid began to inspect the glyphs.

As she looked closer, she realized they *were* Egyptian hieroglyphs. Despite it being worn away by the water's edge, Astrid could read it as plain as day. They had looked so different from afar.

"Yes," she smiled, looking up at Tacama, "They're Egyptian alright." Once she read the message to herself, her hope started to fade. It was a spell, a very ancient one. *Great.* She knew a lot about her own kingdom but she wasn't a priestess; she had no knowledge on how to break ancient spells.

"I'm not sure I like the look on your face." Said Hitomi, walking up behind Astrid. Astrid cursed under her breath.

"There's a reason for that. This is a spell and from the looks of it, this is a pretty powerful one. I have no idea how to break it."

Out of nowhere, Tacama burst into laughter. "A spell 'eh? Whoever built this pyramid is pretty clever; I haven't seen one of those in a long time!"

"What's so funny? People die all the time from these things!"

He rolled his eyes in a childish manner and turned around to look at his mother, a ridiculous grin appearing on his face.

"Remember these things? Scared me to death as a child." He looked back at Astrid, his smile just as big and he sighed gently, "You see Astrid, it's not a real spell. It's just a way of scaring people, to ward off those who don't know any better. It's more of a riddle as it tells you where the key goes. Read it out to me and let's see if we can solve this."

But Astrid was worried as she had been told that people weren't supposed to say spells out loud. What if Tacama was wrong and Astrid curses everyone? But he seemed confident in stating that it's only a mere riddle and he'd seen plenty of these in the past. Astrid just hoped that he was right.

She cleared her throat, still feeling nervous about reciting the message. But she breathed in deeply and began to read.

"The gods of this realm protect their everlasting kingdom with the powers of The River itself. With the wrath of Hapi he shall keep the unwanted away by drowning them beneath the water's edge."

Tacama sat back, trying to hide a grin on his face.

"Oh, now that's a good one! I haven't heard one like that in a long time!"

Astrid looked at him with great confusion, wondering how that could make him smile. "I don't understand..." she muttered.

"Of course you don't - sorry. Like I said before, these messages aren't curses or death threats. They're riddles. The pyramids of each realm are very interesting in the way they're created around the river. You see, getting from the pyramid to the river is quite easy when you have a key but getting from the river to the pyramid is a lot harder. Rather than placing locks and bars to prevent people from entering, keyholes have been hidden for those who possess the key. To find them, you first have to solve the riddle and this one is pretty easy but it's the death threat that scares people."

"...So, where's the keyhole?"

Tacama asked for Astrid's necklace and when she passed it to him, he reached over the boat and stuck his head under the water. A moment and a few bubbles later, he re-emerged, soaking wet. Panting slightly and rubbing his eyes, he regained his composure and smiled at the group.

"That wasn't too hard now. Hitomi, Astrid, come take a look."

Astrid and Hitomi were still quite confused. Both of them peered over the edge of the boat and looked at the water flowing against the wall when suddenly, just below the water's edge, there came a loud cracking sound. The wall began to split in the middle and soon opened up to reveal the most beautiful door Astrid had ever seen.

In all her years she had never seen anything that shimmered so brightly. In the center of the golden door was the Eye of Horus, the symbol was adorned with emerald, sapphire and crimson strokes. It was the sign of peace, protection and the royalty of Egypt.

Home

Tacama grabbed the turquoise handles and pushed open the door. It was pitch dark inside and they were all greeted with the stench of abandonment. He looked back to see their gaze captivated by the darkness.

"Everyone, avert your gaze and I'll light the torches."

They all turned their gaze away from Tacama but Astrid remained frozen in her position. She had heard him quite clearly but her body wouldn't move. She knew that beyond the darkness, Egypt was awaiting her return. She could almost smell the soft warm sand that covered her country like a thick blanket.

With everyone else's head turned, Tacama stepped onto the cold limestone ground and projected fire from his hands, lighting up the inside of the Egyptian pyramid. He then launched flames towards the dusty torches, setting them alight, giving life to the abandoned structure.

They all turned their heads as they noticed the fire glowing within the doorway and as they looked through the opening, they were truly amazed by what they saw. The interior of this pyramid was vastly different to the one in Tolico. It was made up of shimmering limestone bricks, each one a different shade of amber and crimson. As the fire shone near the walls they glistened brightly like stardust.

Straight ahead of Tacama lay a long corridor which was considerably wide. On either side were incredibly large stone statues that stretched from floor to ceiling. From what Astrid could see, they were statues of Egyptian men and women in ancient garb. They looked like guardians of the pyramid.

"Torches are lit and everything is packed," said Tacama, turning back to everyone. "Ready to go?"

Xoco grabbed the bag of essentials and with Tacama's help she was lifted from the boat and onto the lit platform. Next was Tepin, who glared at Tacama when he offered her some assistance. Astrid's cat, Nefert - who had been sleeping until then - leapt onto the platform with one swift bound, making sure to keep away from the water as he crouched between Tepin's ankles.

As Tacama looked at Hitomi and waited for her to stand, her body trembled and her breath quickened. But she rose from the boat and looked at Astrid, as if to wait for her approval. Astrid smiled in return, knowing that Hitomi just needed a little push to feel comfortable. She then leapt onto the platform and stood beside Xoco, giving just enough room for Astrid to arrive safely.

With a sigh of nervousness, Astrid grabbed her bag, secured it over her shoulder and then stood up from her seat. Tacama stretched out his hand to guide her.

"Ready to go home, Princess?" He smiled. Astrid took his hand and jumped onto the platform. Making sure she was safely within the pyramid.

Astrid looked up at Tacama and the others and said, "Yes... yes I am."

As they made their way along the corridor, Hitomi walked closely with Astrid, almost as if she was glued to her side. But it seemed rational as she was now in another foreign realm and deep into the unknown. She seemed to ease up as she gazed upon the pyramid. It was much smaller and less complex than the Tolico pyramid, but it was so beautiful. Astrid seemed more preoccupied with the large statues that stood guard along the corridor, it brought to mind statues she had seen before in Abu Simbel.

What if we're in the temple of Abu Simbel? No, that

can't be right, I would have remembered the statues and they weren't nearly as odd as these.

Getting more curious about these sculptures, she looked at Tacama and wondered if he knew anything about them.

"Tacama, do you know who these statues are meant to resemble?" She asked at last.

Tacama paused for a moment and glanced up at the enormous figures. He glanced at each one of them before stopping at the one nearest him. He nudged Xoco and nodded towards it.

"Well?" Astrid repeated.

"They are all special people. All of them are old and famous gatekeepers of the realms, serving to protect and guard the pyramids of the kingdoms. I recognize a few of them. This one," he said as he pointed to a statue of a man dressed in a linen wrap, his attire was modest and he almost managed to blend in with the others, if it wasn't for his soft - yet familiar - appearance.

"This is my father, probably the most famous of the gate keepers."

Astrid was stunned, she felt bad for not recognizing the statue that clearly possessed features recognizable in Tacama, almost like she was looking at a slightly older version of the new king. It seemed clear now that he took after his father; from the silly grin to the firm and strong stance. Both his father - in his younger years - and Tacama alike had attempted a look of strength but their gentler expression had appeared to seep through their tough exterior.

"After we get you home, I can tell you all about these people." Tacama continued, leading the group forward. He looked ahead and noticed something. "I can see just by the door, there are a few empty spaces, waiting for other gatekeepers. Perhaps it's waiting for you Astrid, to become a part of this great legacy. This pyramid looks abandoned and there's probably a good forty years of dust here so you may want to find someone to look after it. It'd be nice to see a giant statue of you standing next to all of these folk."

The thought of becoming a gatekeeper for Egypt was overwhelming for Astrid. But she was interested in hearing the stories that Tacama knew about these people. Astrid noticed that Tacama seemed preoccupied with the statue beside his father, a man whose robe was fluent and free like the wind.

Astrid's curiosity could not remain silent and she asked Tacama if he knew this man as well.

"That's a conversation for a later time." Said Tacama as they began to arrive at the end of the corridor. "There are more important things to get done now." He gently pushed Astrid towards the closed entrance that stood before them. In a low tone he said to Astrid, "Princess would you do us the honor of opening the door?"

Astrid laughed under her breath. It took her a while to realize that after all this time, she was *actually* in Egypt and within a few moments she'd be home. All she had to do was open the door.

The sunshine had never felt so good against her face. She missed the warmth and brightness of the Egyptian climate, embracing all in its welcoming light. The warm golden sand stretched far ahead and just on the horizon was the most beautiful thing Astrid had ever seen in her entire life - the palace of Luxor.

Wait, she thought, *if the pyramid was this close to the temple to begin with, then why have I never seen it before?*

She looked over her shoulder for a moment to see the crumbled remains of the pyramid that they just came from. It looked more like a sand pile than any sort of pyramid she'd ever seen, but Astrid finally recognized it. As a child, her father would bring her here and she would play with the daughters and sons of many nobles. In fact, she had climbed to the top of this 'pyramid' more times than she could possibly count. If only her younger self knew what this sand pile held within it.

Suddenly, their peaceful silence was broken by the sound of yelling from coming from behind them. They turned to see a man riding on horseback emerge around the ruins of the pyramid. He seemed to appear from nowhere, armed with a sword and an expression that said he was prepared to use it. The party instantly prepared to defend themselves.

But Astrid recognized the rider, she knew him, it was her father's right-hand man, Seth. As he got closer to the group, Astrid was happy and relieved to see a familiar face after so long.

"Your majesty!" The man yelled in surprise, stopping his horse in its tracks. "You have returned to us! We have been looking for you everywhere! Wait, who are these people?" He dismounted and unsheathed his blade. Without hesitation, he pointed his sword at Tacama, "Are you the ones who kidnapped my princess!?"

Even though he was only nineteen and his face was gentle Astrid knew that no one messed with him and those who did would quickly regret it. He was one of the greatest fighters Egypt had ever seen and he could only be beaten by the king himself.

Without thinking, Astrid stood in front of Tacama and was now an inch away from Seth's blade, meeting his concerned look with a stern one of her own.

"No, they're my friends. My kidnapper is long gone thanks to them. I will only order you one time to put down your weapon and swear that should you need to use it, it will be to defend these people. Do you understand?"

Astrid surprised herself, she had never ordered anyone in that tone before. *Gods, I sounded just like father!* And from the look of it, Seth was surprised to hear Astrid speak in such a way, but he knew better than to question the princess. Astrid and Seth had always managed to stay on the same track, knowing what the other was thinking and vice versa.

"Of course, Your Highness," he said, sheathing his sword and bowing from the waist. "My apologies to you and your companions."

The group, feeling assured that Astrid had things under control, could see that they could lower their guard. Hitomi came into view, feeling embarrassed that she had hid behind Xoco like a shy child. Astrid took her hand and after a few moments of briefly explaining to Seth about her and her friends, she asked him to take them to the palace.

Knowing that it would be best not to ask questions, Seth looked toward the surrounding dunes, cupped his hands to his face and whistled. Instantly on hearing his call a group of guards appeared who had clearly been waiting to be summoned. Once more Astrid had to explain that her friends meant no harm and should be offered every protection and the utmost hospitality; they were soon led toward the palace.

Infancy

Inside, the palace was abnormally quiet, the guards weren't at their posts. Astrid's heart skipped a beat, she feared that something terrible had happened. She knew that it wasn't a trap, there was nothing to fear here but she knew something was wrong.

"Is the palace always this empty?" Muttered Hitomi, inching her way closer to Astrid. For once, Astrid wasn't able to answer a question about her home. She looked toward Seth, who didn't seem to be all that concerned about the absence of people.

Instead, he merely kept walking forward, assuming that everyone would follow him. When he didn't hear the sound of footsteps behind, he turned immediately and looked at Astrid with concern, worried that something was wrong.

"Your highness?" He asked.

Astrid stepped back toward the door, fear seeping into her mind.

"Where is everyone?" She called out nervously. "The guards? Servants? Where are they?"

Seth understood and looked ashamed to have not told her sooner. He tried to calm her down.

"Your highness, forgive me for not telling you sooner. During your absence, the queen - your mother gave birth to a baby boy. The servants are caring for them both and the guards are keeping the royal family safe."

After hearing the news, Astrid almost fell over with relief. The group smiled at hearing the news and Xoco and Tepin hugged Astrid.

"That is where I was taking you, I assumed you wanted to see your parents without delay. Am I wrong?"

Astrid could barely find the words to speak. Her mother had given birth while she was missing. *I have a little brother.* Noticing that Astrid was still a bit shaken, Xoco came beside her and rested a hand on her shoulder.

"She's fine," she whispered as she kissed the top of Astrid's head. As they began to follow Seth, Xoco kept reassuring Astrid that her mother and baby brother were OK.

The group approached a room that was heavily guarded by some of Egypt's greatest knights. The moment they saw Seth approaching with a group of strangers in tow, they instinctively unsheathed their swords and were ready to attack. But when they saw Astrid walking towards them, the knights were petrified at the sight of their missing princess. One of them looked frantic and bowed immediately before Astrid, whilst the others guards stood in disbelief with their swords still poised. The bowing guard looked at Seth in shock, demanding answers immediately.

Seth quickly shushed him and walked to his side, whispering to him, "I will explain everything to you soon. But first, you must let the princess see her family."

The guard nodded and the others, realizing their mistake, quickly sheathed their swords and were soon bowing as well.

The group agreed to stay outside for a while, allowing Astrid to have a few moments alone with her family.

The thought of seeing her parents after so long filled her with anxiety. She couldn't understand why as she had been longing to see them ever since she was taken. Nervously, she walked toward the door, knocking gently and then slowly opening it.

Her father, Thutamun didn't even seem to notice her presence and her mother, Nefatarin was completely enthused with a little bundle tucked into her arms.

"Mother? Father?" Astrid whispered, her chest clenching in excitement.

Thutamun looked up for a millisecond before looking back down. It only took him a moment to realize what he had just seen. His expression had changed completely and he looked up, realizing that his missing daughter stood before him. With his mouth agape, he began to tremble slightly. He then leapt up from shock.

Nefatarin looked at her husband in astonishment, cradling the baby slightly tighter. She then saw Astrid standing before them. She remained silent and surprised, not knowing how to react, but her eyes spoke volumes on her behalf as tears flowed and the biggest smile of relief broke across her face.

Thutamun ran towards Astrid. She didn't even see him move but was soon engulfed in the warmth of her father's embrace as he lifted her from the floor and hugged her so hard he was in danger of suffocating his daughter. Astrid was overjoyed at the feeling of strength of her father's arms securely around her. He buried his face in her hair and she buried her face in his chest, not wanting to ever be away from him again.

"My girl," he cried out. "My baby girl, oh gods I thought you were gone. I thought you were gone forever."

The next few hours were quite rushed as so many things were happening at once. There were many questions and many answers. She was praised, over and over again, told countless times how proud they were, but she couldn't accept their praise as she felt she didn't deserve it.

Astrid had lied, everyone lied about the majority of events that took place in Tolico. She knew how upset her mother would be if she knew that Astrid had been a part of a rebellion and fought against the man who had killed thousands of people. Nefatarin would have gone mad from just hearing that her daughter went up against a deadly assassin.

Instead, Tacama told her parents an alternative version of events in which he had saved both Hitomi and Astrid, heroically killed Moha and took his throne. Short, simple and believable, and no mention of a rebellion whatsoever. If Nefatarin believed it, then no one had anything to worry about, even though it was quite obvious that Thutamun doubted most of it. Astrid would have plenty of time later to tell him the truth.

As their conversation came to an end, arrangements had been made so that everyone would be able to stay in Egypt for as long as they needed, with Nefatarin saying, "It's important that you get plenty of rest. You all need to able to get home safely and we will supply you with anything that you may need for the journey." Thutamun led everyone out of the study where they had spoken without interruption and then handed them over to a young servant named Rey, the handmaiden of Astrid.

Realizing that everyone was being rushed away, Astrid hadn't had a chance to speak or ask any of the questions that were spinning through her mind. But before she could say a word, her baby brother was soon placed in her arms. She was soon left alone with her mother and new brother.

Nefatarin gave her daughter a quick hug, a kiss on the head, and just barely above a coherent whisper, she said, "I want you to name him for me, something brave and heroic, huh? Thank you darling."

She left Astrid and practically danced her way to the rest of the group.

Astrid then remembered something important that couldn't wait till morning or for a moment longer.

"Wait! Hold on! I've got questions, ones that can't wait through another storytelling." Astrid yelled, her voice carried through the echoes of the palace. Suddenly, everyone in the group turned to look in her direction. She rushed forward, taking care not to disturb her baby brother. She pushed her way between Xoco and her father and grabbed Hitomi's hand.

"She has no home." Astrid said, looking back at her parents. Everyone paused, probably hoping Astrid could bring up the topic later, but she continued. "Hitomi is all by herself now and has no home to return to. I don't want her to be all alone, to be deserted while I'm safe at home. Her kingdom, her family were all taken by Moha. We're all she has left..."

Before either parent could reply, Tacama came behind Astrid, resting his hand on her shoulder and saying in agreement, "She's right you know. I may have a kingdom of my own but Hitomi will only be seen and treated as a mere guest. She will have no parents, no right to a kingdom that deserves her. I'd hope she may be able to settle for a life here with her friend, with people that will love her as their own."

The hallway was silent for a moment, only to be disturbed by the footsteps of passing servants and guards. After what seemed an eternity, Thutamun looked at her daughter, hugging her for the umpteenth time.

"I appreciate that you and King Tacama have brought this to my attention..." he sighed and then his face broke into a bright smile, mimicking the one Astrid always seemed to give. "I would never let a royal child go without a kingdom. If my wife and I can bring a new child into Egypt, there is no reason why we cannot bring in another. We'll have a celebration for Astrid's return and for the birth of my new son. We will also arrange a coronation for our arrival and it will be an event to remember. How does that sound?"

Astrid was almost knocked over as Hitomi through her

arms around her friend. Perhaps she would have if she hadn't had an infant in her arms. But Astrid was happy to see Hitomi beaming with joy.

"How can I ever repay you?" She whispered, wiping away tears forming around her eyes.

Astrid grinned up at her parents whilst adjusting her little brother in her arms. Looking at them both, she couldn't help but smile and said gently, "Thank you." She then looked at her mother, saying eagerly, "Mother, I've managed to pick a name for him." She looked up at Tacama, who was grinning more than ever. "Tacama."

Both Tacama and Nefatarin looked a little puzzled, wondering if Astrid had suddenly gone off topic. Noticing everyone's confusion, she realized she had to correct herself and said, "No, no that's the name I chose, Tacama. Mother, you said you wanted a name that shows bravery. Well, why not give him the name of the bravest man I know?"

Her parents looked at each other and agreed to the name while Tacama looked as though he may just cry at the thought of a child being named after him.

As everyone was escorted to their own rooms, Astrid couldn't help but worry about Hitomi being alone in her chamber. She began to think of Hitomi more as a sister than a friend and she smiled to herself, happy at the fact that Hitomi would be a part of the family. But she wasn't the only one who was worried. Astrid nodded off to sleep but awoke a short while later with Hitomi sleeping soundly beside her.

"You're as clingy as the cat." She chuckled and pulled more of her blanket over Hitomi. She paused, her hand still over her sister's arm. Hitomi didn't appear to be asleep. Her eyes were still closed and she didn't react to Astrid moving in bed but she definitely wasn't asleep.

Astrid sighed, "What's wrong?" She asked. It was

obvious that Hitomi knew she was caught. She groaned as she turned on her back and rubbed her tired eyes.

"Sorry." She muttered.

"For what?"

"For worrying you."

There was a moment of silence before Hitomi sat up. She took Astrid's hand in her own and let out a heavy sigh.

"I'm thankful that you let me stay here and that your parents wanted me. I'm glad that everyone is happy… But for some reason I just don't feel like I deserve it. I guess I thought I was going to live in that shack for the rest of my life and now that I'm not there anymore, I just…"

"Don't think about that." Astrid said gently. "You deserved more than a shack in the woods and I'm not the only one who thinks that way. You can't let yourself become consumed with doubt. You deserve a home, a family, a kingdom, and peace. All of us do, but you most of all." She quietly laughed and said, "And most of all, we deserve some sleep. We've got a big day tomorrow, it's going to be great, I promise."

Gods and Monsters

Astrid's heartbeat grew in excitement with every second. She couldn't believe that today was the day that Hitomi would be welcomed into their family and recognized as a princess in Egypt. Both of them were told to sit on their assigned thrones and to keep their heads bowed. Astrid snuck a look at Hitomi and smiled at her, amazed at how Hitomi was waiting patiently for the priest to arrive while the crowd prayed to the gods.

She couldn't help but smile at how rigid Hitomi looked, stiffly sitting in the chair and waiting for it all to be over. She kept fidgeting in her seat, probably worrying that she was doing something wrong. And she couldn't help but fidget in her new robes, feeling like a dressed up doll that was waiting to be adored. But she looked beautiful in Egyptian clothes; she almost looked like an entirely different person, especially with her face covered in ceremonial colors.

Astrid laughed under her breath at her friend's nervousness, she reached over, taking Hitomi's clammy hand in her own.

"Relax," Astrid whispered. "It'll be fine."

Behind her, Astrid heard the priest talking to someone, telling him to make sure that everything was ready. She knew that the ceremony was about to begin. She enjoyed Egyptian ceremonies as they would always take place outside of the mighty temples of their ancestors, for them to look down and bless them. After a moment, the priest stopped speaking in the religious tongue and the crowd raised their heads from praying.

"An award of bravery," the priest called out, "is given today to the princess of Egypt."

The crowd erupted into a thundering applause. Astrid did her best to stay still and to look out at the people, but she ached with anxiety, almost as if she didn't want to be awarded. She wasn't exactly sure why the thought of the priest placing the necklace around her neck made her so nervous, she hadn't been at all nervous beforehand. Whatever it was, it made Astrid more jumpy than ever, almost urging her to run and leave the ceremony immediately.

Just as she thought her heart couldn't take any more, she suddenly saw the priest's hands come up in front of her, a necklace gripped tightly between his fingers. She was surprised by how beautiful the necklace was. Astrid had noticed over the years how ceremonial jewelry only looked beautiful from a distance.

But this necklace was different, like it had been especially designed for her. It was made from segments of malachite and onyx, each segment shaped like a delicate teardrop which encircled a small symbol of the Eye of Horus. The most peculiar thing about it was that it had an engraving on the back of the pendant. She turned it slightly and saw her name. Astrid had never seen a cartouche of her own name and the sight of it immediately dissolved her anxieties. She knew the significance of having your name as a cartouche as it was only done for warriors and heroes. The people of Egypt now saw her not as just a pretty princess, but as a hero.

She closed her eyes and let the priest place the necklace around her neck. After he moved away from her, Astrid looked back at Hitomi who was now tightly gripping Astrid's hand. The priest then walked over to Hitomi who looked up at him anxiously.

"The kingdom of Egypt recognizes the princess of

Japan as the daughter of our pharaoh and queen, a princess of Egypt." The priest called out as he raised a golden circlet above Hitomi's head.

Astrid tenderly squeezed Hitomi's hand back, letting her know that it would be all right. The priest let out another booming set of chants and finally placed the crown onto Hitomi's head.

The crowd once again fell into silence and began to pray. Hitomi looked at Astrid with an expression of confusion.

"Do I pray again?" She whispered. Astrid shook her head and smiled.

"Just enjoy the silence for a moment." However, the silence did not last for more than a few seconds. Amongst the people there came the sound of someone clapping. Everyone looked up, whispering their shock at the noise and wondering who the culprit was.

"Who dares to interrupt the ceremony?" The priest roared in fury. The clapping continued and it began to get louder, almost as if the culprit was coming towards the stage. Astrid's father stood from his throne and reached for his sword.

At last, the perpetrators revealed themselves. They were all masked; the leader was hidden behind three men who shoved people aside as they strode toward Astrid and Hitomi. The leader emerged, followed by an elderly man who possessed such a deathly glare.

"Oh, am I interrupting?" The leader gasped mockingly. "I'm so sorry! I waited until everyone was quiet so I could speak. That's not interrupting, that's being patient. But it was very rude of you to yell so loudly." Everyone looked on with confusion, wondering who this person could be.

"Oh! Where are my manners? Let me just take this silly thing off so that we can talk properly." As the leader took the mask off, Astrid's heart sank.

Gods have mercy, she thought as she looked up at her

father.

"You are not welcome here, Moha!" Thutamun growled as he raised his sword into a fighting stance. Instantly, Tacama, Xoco, and Tepin jumped from their seats and ran to Hitomi and Astrid. Seth also ran to their side and was accompanied by a group of royal guards. They all stood in front of Astrid and Hitomi, wielding their weapons and ready to fight. Moha let out a hearty laugh and clamped an arm around one of his companions.

The elderly man near Moha began to look more familiar and as she focused on him, she soon realized who it was and she was speechless. The others soon realized who he was as well and Xoco's eyes were filled with horror. It was Cacama.

"Not welcome?" Moha bellowed. "That's funny Thutamun, I remember you once saying that I was always welcome. You weren't lying were you?" He let out a deep sigh and began to focus on a young boy within the crowd who was hiding behind his mother. "Lying is such a filthy habit, isn't it, your highness?" Moha purred. "Lying can seriously hurt others and sometimes, it can kill them." He grabbed a dagger from his waist and threw it at the child, striking him in the forehead. The boy went limp and fell back with a heavy thud. The mother shrieked in horror and embraced her dead child.

The crowd erupted into panic, the desert was filled with the screams of horror and many of the people began to run.

"After them!" Moha said fiercely to his men. He then turned his attention back towards the royal family. "Now that we have some peace and quiet!" He yelled over the screams of the crowd, "how about we have a civilized talk?"

"You dare hurt one of my people!?" Thutamun roared in anger and he leapt off of the stage, running to confront Moha.

Moha let out another laugh and asked scornfully, "You dare fight me?"

Thutamun grit his teeth and nodded, raising his sword towards his foe's neck. Moha stepped forward and gripped the neck of the sword. Blood flowed from his hand and a demented grin emerged on his lips. "I did not come to fight you, I came to fight the misfits." He said in a hoarse voice.

Underneath Astrid's robes was her Azuli sword, strapped around her thigh in its small form. Without thinking, Astrid grabbed her weapon and strapped it onto her hand but before she could activate it, the sound of a shrill scream caused her to freeze. It was her mother. She turned towards her father and hoped that her doubts were wrong.

Thutamun dropped his sword and glanced down at his torso to find a thin arrow that had penetrated his solar plexus. Cacama came forward with a bow in hand and gripped Thutamun by the shoulder before shoving him to the ground.

"Father!" Astrid screamed in horror. She activated her blade and jumped off the stage.

Tacama quickly grabbed her around the waist and yanked her backwards. "Wait!" He hissed. "It's a trap!"

Astrid tried to break free from Tacama's grip, desperate to go to her father's side. But she also knew that Tacama might be right. However, her mother began to run, shoving her way past Tepin and Seth and she sprinted down the stairs before either one of them could catch her.

"Thutamun!" She sobbed as she ran towards her husband. Moha reached forward and grabbed her by her hair. She shrieked loudly in pain.

"Not so fast." He whispered, jabbing a blade into her stomach. Astrid eyes widened. She was now consumed with rage and this time, no one stopped Astrid from running. The group followed her, weapons in hand.

"Gods damn it, Moha!" Tacama bellowed as he threw

his sword up and pointed it at his brother's neck. "You leave them out of this! If you want to kill anyone then kill me! I'm the one you want! Just stop this, don't kill another person!"

Moha looked at Tacama with disgust, outraged that he would speak to him in such a tone.

Tacama glanced over at Astrid, saying to her quickly, "Go to your parents."

Astrid did not need persuading and rushed forward. She knelt beside her mother, turning her face away from Moha and hoping that Tacama could keep his brother at bay for a moment.

But it seemed impossible to keep Moha still. He fought all four of them along with the Egyptian guards with such abnormal strength and quick reflexes. For a moment, Astrid thought Cacama was right, maybe Moha was a demon and maybe demons can't be killed. She looked back to her mother, her fear getting the best of her but she tried her best to put on a brave face.

"It's alright mother, you'll be OK." Astrid whispered, pushing the stray hairs away from her mother's damp face. Nefatarin weakly grabbed for her daughter's hand and made Astrid power down her sword.

"Look at you," she said faintly, "look at you. Just like your father." She looked over at Moha and Tacama who were in the middle of a heated battle. "You should be helping them." She looked back at her daughter and mumbled, "Forgive me Astrid."

"Forgive you for what?!" Astrid barked as panic welled up inside her. "Don't say things like that!"

Nefatarin choked out a laugh, her breaths getting shorter with every minute. "I am sorry for underestimating you. I thought you weren't capable of such things. You're my baby girl Astrid, but you're also a warrior. You need to save Egypt, you need to save our people Astrid."

Astrid shook her head, tears streaking her cheeks and falling onto her mother's face. "I'm not going to leave you here!"

Nefatarin's face turned grim and angry. "No Astrid, there's no saving me. You have to be brave, for me and your f...father. Go fight for your kingdom and for your family! Go!"

Astrid let out a heavy breath and nodded, her mother was right. She couldn't let herself stay here and she couldn't hide. "I love you," she whispered, softly kissing Nefatarin's forehead and placing her head gently on the ground.

She stood up from her mother's side and powered her sword. She ran toward the fight.

"Stop hiding behind your brother, Moha!" She yelled, "Come and fight your real enemy!"

There was a brief moment of silence as Moha turned toward Astrid and pointed his blade in her direction. A disgusting growl sputtered from his lips. The sight of him was repulsive, like a mad dog seething with insanity. But in that moment, Astrid heard a laugh from behind her, her mother's laugh. But it was soon consumed by silence.

Anger grew in her chest, Astrid was through with hiding and most of all, she was done with people attacking those she loved. Her parents were dead and she couldn't hide behind them anymore. If she continued to hide in fear, everyone she loved would soon be gone.

"Are you going to just stand there like a shy child?" She snarled as she stepped towards Moha. Moha remained hesitant, refusing to play along with her tricks. "What? Do you think Tacama is going to stab you in the back when you're not looking? Do you think he'd really do that? Well, he's not a coward who will strike an opponent when they're not looking. Unlike you."

That immediately grabbed Moha's attention. He lowered his blade and started walking towards her. Out of the corner of Astrid's eye, she saw Cacama inch up behind Tacama with a dagger in hand.

"Behind you!" She yelled. Tacama looked around and punched Cacama in the stomach, removing his dagger and pushing him to the ground. For a moment, the crisis was diverted, until she turned back to see a blade to her neck. She could feel the cool edge of sharp metal near her skin.

How had he managed to move so quickly? That wasn't the only question Astrid had. *How is he alive? How did he get to Egypt? What the hell is happening!?*

"Never turn your back on your opponent, you ignorant child." Moha sneered, pressing the blade harder against Astrid's skin.

He had a good point, she had to admit that. Not even a minute into their duel and Moha already had a fatal blow ready. His stance was too strong and there were no weak points for Astrid to hit. He was like a solid block of marble, there was nothing Astrid could do...

'For all I know, this new found ability can be a great asset to you." Astrid recalled Tacama's wise words before his coronation and she had nearly forgotten about what she was capable of, a supernatural ability that was flowing through her veins.

Astrid looked directly into the dark dead eyes of Moha, causing him to flinch ever so slightly. Gods, they mimicked the eyes of a beast, no wonder his people thought he was a demon. But Astrid hadn't been defeated just yet.

"You haven't won, Moha." She sneered and without touching the blade, it abruptly moved away from her, making it look like it had slipped. She pushed him away and regained her balance, arming herself once more with her Azuli sword.

Despite the fact that Astrid had managed to get away, Moha remained confident.

"Haven't won?" Moha laughed loudly. "It's a little too

soon to decide the fate of this battle." He swung his sword forward with great force but Astrid dodged his attack with her own blade.

In this heated battle, she was barely able to look around to see if her friends were dead or alive. But the thought of them dead made her feel sick, she'd rather look at Moha with that terrifying, brutal grin than to see the lifeless bodies of her friends and family. She found it difficult to avoid his strikes as his sheer strength was enough to end her. She needed to remain swift and agile.

She spun around, avoiding a blow to the shoulder and in that moment, she caught a glimpse of her surroundings. The golden sand beneath her feet was damp and tainted with blood. The desert had been peppered with death; corpses were scattered all around and amongst the dead she saw her mother and father, lying still on the sand. It was as if everyone was sleeping on a golden blanket. The smell of death now lingered in the air, the stench was overwhelming in the heat. They were all innocent, they had nothing to do with this and yet they were killed.

She kept moving back, making sure that Moha focused on her alone. In the distance, she saw Tacama fighting against one of Moha's men and Hitomi looked like a moth against a mantis, her robes torn, her blade barely visible. Xoco and Tepin were nowhere to be found, but she prayed they were still alive.

Out of nowhere, she heard Tacama yell, "Behind you!" She dodged left and swung around to see Cacama swinging a sword at her. He was one of the last people she wanted to fight. Cacama looked at Moha for a moment and nodded.

"What are you doing?" Astrid yelled at Cacama, slamming her blade against his. "You were supposed to be on our side!"

He scoffed, "I told you Astrid, you cannot kill a demon

like Moha and look what happened, he's alive! You can't fight him, it's impossible! You need to learn a lesson, you can't destroy a god!"

As the sun shone brightly on the dead, Moha let out a sigh of relief and was able to relax for a moment. As he looked out at the desert and admired his little war zone, he grinned at the countless people that died on his account. His mother was lying unconscious on the sand and Tacama was growing weaker by the moment. Tepin was nowhere to be found and Astrid would soon be taken down by Cacama. As for Hitomi, he'd have to take care of her by himself.

She may have been young, but it was apparent to Moha that wherever she had been hiding over the last few years, she had plenty of time to practice the art of the sword. He had never seen anyone fight so… beautifully. He would soon fix that but there were more important things to take care of first.

As he walked towards the pharaohs' throne, he found behind it the body of a servant. He admired his men's handiwork, the ability of killing someone swiftly and not a single drop of blood would be found; but that was only when they felt like it. Suddenly, he heard something cry.

Still secured tightly in her limp arms, he found the form of an infant. Moha looked back at Nefatarin, noting that her belly was far less full than it was when he had met her initially. He knelt down to the infant, moving the pale green fabric from his face. The baby looked like Thutamun, dark hair and pale brown eyes. He laughed at how the baby cried in the same way his mother did when his father was killed.

I have to destroy them all, don't I? He mused. *This child is related to that brat, he'll know one day about what had happened here. Never again will there be a repeat of this nonsense.*

And so he raised his sword once more and quickly

ended a life that had just begun.

"Astrid! Turn around!" Cried Xoco from afar. She couldn't see her but she had assumed that whatever danger was lurking in front of her was also being shrouded by the sun. She spun about, guarding her back with her sword and winced, hoping whatever was happening would end quickly. Unfortunately... it did. Out of nowhere, cutting through the sound of clashing swords came an odd wallop as something hit the sand.

After a moment, Xoco came up behind her, resting a hand on her shoulder, her breath shaky with exhaustion.

"Don't turn around, Astrid, just keep fighting, don't look over here and don't worry about Cacama, you understand?" Astrid didn't know how to respond to that. What was so bad that Xoco didn't want Astrid to see? What did she just do? "Do you understand me!" She barked, her soft fingertips suddenly clawing into Astrid's shoulder.

At last, with a gulp of anxiety, she nodded and once Xoco let go of her she ran forward, throwing herself back into the battle.

"You think killing Cacama is going to solve anything?" Came a voice from behind Xoco. She turned around and faced her son, looking him dead in the eye.

She shook her head and said, "No Moha. At least, not for you." Moha laughed and looked past Xoco, taking a long good look at the remains of his uncle.

"That was very courageous of you, beheading your own little brother. I'll make sure that your bravery does not go unnoticed."

Astrid looked around for the others once more. Hitomi was still fighting and she finally saw Tepin, alive. But where was Tacama? She lowered her blade for a moment, looking towards the horizon, praying she would see him soon. Suddenly, something grabbed her foot from below and she jumped, ready to make strike.

"Astrid!" Hissed a voice. Before she could do anything, she was dragged down to the sand. Astrid twisted and kicked at whatever was grabbing her, trying to make it loosen its grip on her. Finally, her body began to tire and after a moment she wiped her brow, feeling defeated as she looked at the enemy.

But it was no enemy at all, it was Tacama. His body half buried in the sand, he winced with pain, his body covered in dozens of cuts and bruises. He let go of her ankle, his arm feeling sore and numb from her kicking.

"You need to keep your blade raised no matter what!" He muttered angrily, trying his best to ignore the pain and give Astrid an angry glare. He attempted to sit up but it seemed that gravity would not let him escape its grasp.

Astrid leaned over him and searched for any fatal wounds. To her relief she found none, but why was he in so much pain? What had happened to him?

"Listen," Tacama growled, wiping the bloodied sand from his cheek, "I got hit hard on my back so I'm useless right now. Don't worry, I don't think it's serious, just can't move a damn thing." He reached for his head but Astrid stopped him, grabbing his hand tightly in her own.

"Don't say you're fine when you're clearly not." Her eyes were downcast and it looked like she had given up.

He sighed, rolling his eyes in displeasure and tried to reassure her, "For the gods' sake Astrid, I'm fine. But I won't lie to you, I can't fight right now. Also, I need to tell you something, it's important. You probably doubt me in seeing Moha alive but I swear to you Astrid, I killed him. My blade went straight through his heart, I felt it come out the other side. I don't know how he survived so you'll need to be extremely careful. I know you were fighting him for a moment and I have a feeling that it won't be the last time.

You need to know the weak points of his fighting skills. He possesses an unnatural skill with a sword, it's almost impossible to find a weak spot on him, but I know one. As a child, he fell down a hill and broke his left leg. Even now it bothers him, so if you need a quick getaway, kick his left knee. You will gain some distance from him." He groaned, turning his head slightly to look over at Hitomi.

After a moment, he looked back at Astrid, a cheeky grin began to creep its way onto his face surprisingly. "I saw you fighting him and I know you'll be able to beat him. But you're at a disadvantage, you're skills show me that you're meant to fight with two blades, I can tell. Take mine," he nodded towards his side where his own sword lay almost buried in the sand. "You're a natural fighter Astrid, I can tell."

Astrid froze, she didn't like the way he was talking, she didn't like the way he wanted her to have his sword. She still found herself reaching for his blade. Although, when she wrapped her fingers around the handle, he grabbed her hand again.

"Don't give me that look," he said with his brows furrowing. "I told you I will be fine and I mean it. I won't die, not now, not for a long time and neither will you. I didn't want this to happen, I'm sorry but I can't do anything now. I can only tell you to fight, so do exactly that."

Astrid let out a shaky sigh, nodded solemnly before rising up. She turned away from him and quickly scanned the area for Moha. She stood still for a moment, quickly testing what it felt like to wield two blades, to feel their weight in each hand. Even though she was ready with two swords firmly grasped, she was holding back.

She felt like she was still hiding in this battle, even when she told herself she wouldn't. Astrid knew Moha wasn't going to stop unless he was forced to. She looked around at the countless people lying in the sand. Many were dead, her parents were dead and Tacama lay severely injured.

As far as she could tell, she was almost the last one standing on the desert, the last one able to fight. Xoco was nowhere to be found and Hitomi was busy taking down guards like flies. All of the Egyptian knights were either dead or on the brink of death.

She looked down at Tacama's weapon. It mimicked the beautiful craftsmanship and elegance of the Azuli sword. She then looked down at herself, she had dozens of cuts and scratches across her arms, her legs and chest. Her necklace was badly damaged, it was missing large segments and it hung by a thread. She saw that she still looked like a feeble little princess, all dressed up in her jewels and long white robes. She wasn't really prepared for battle.

Before any of Moha's men could attack her, she took her blade to her dress and tore off a good length of the hem until it set just above her knees. She removed all of her jewelry, apart from her lapis pendant and then walked towards one of the dead Egyptian knights.

She didn't like the idea of raiding a corpse but she had no choice. She removed his breastplate and strapped it onto her own chest. She used a piece of suede from around his wrist to wrap up her hair. Now she felt ready to do battle. She was finished with people fighting for her, now it was time for her to fight for the people she cared for most.

Astrid caught sight of Moha, who was sitting upon her father's throne, looking down at the ongoing battle as though it was a play being put on just for him. She gripped her blades tighter and ran toward him.

"Moha!" She yelled out. "Taking a break already?" He looked down at her and laughed.

Lazily he stood reached for his sword. He sighed and yawned before leaping down from the platform.

"Of course," he mocked. "Watching people die while

you barely do any work is boring, I needed a rest after hearing all those people whine and squirm. It's very tiring."

He spun his sword around repeatedly; his faux exhaustion faded quickly and was soon replaced with frightening determination. "So Astrid, do you mind if I make this battle quick?"

Astrid gritted her teeth and raised both swords. "The less I have to look at your disgusting face, the better Moha," she growled. He paused and dropped his sword to the ground, looking slightly confused.

"Really?" He asked. "Well, if you insist. Then let me at least use my favorite blade." He reached for his waist and pulled out his obsidian dagger. "It was so nice of Xoco to let me have this back. I think it's quite a nice touch to kill you with the blade that has slaughtered all of the other blue-eyed beasts like you."

Astrid refused to respond, which surprisingly bothered him. He was getting more frustrated by the minute. Much like Astrid, he was done fighting and he was ready to put this pathetic attempt of a rebellion to rest. He walked toward her, taking long strides while glaring like the god of death himself.

"I have plans Astrid, very big plans," he held up his arm, revealing the odd set of tattoos that Astrid had seen the first day she met him. "I have created the Opress and with it, I will be able to get anything I desire. But you're in my way and I can't let that happen. I can't let you destroy me now, big things are happening and I won't allow you to interfere!"

A demonic laugh erupted from Moha as he came closer to Astrid. She swallowed her anxiety and clenched her Azuli sword tightly. She felt more powerful as her skin squeezed the hilts of her swords.

Moha's head cocked to the side and a sadistic grin formed on his bloodied lips. "Now, did you really think you could get away from me?" He lulled in a smooth monotone voice. "How stupid of you, Astrid. This is all your fault; you should have listened to me. Perhaps if you listened, your family and friends would not be dead. The sand wouldn't be soaking in the blood of your people. But now you have to pay; now you have to suffer for your ignorance. You'll discover the true wrath of the Opress!"

Without warning, Moha threw his dagger at Astrid with immense force. Astrid's heart stopped and fear pulsed through her veins as the weapon flew toward her. She closed her eyes and waited for the dagger to strike.

"What?!"

Astrid opened her eyes at Moha's outrage. She soon found Moha's dagger floating a few inches from her face. Moha was frozen stiff in shock, unable to comprehend what was happening. Astrid's heart beat harder and her hands shook. What was she supposed to do? Moha wouldn't be stunned for long.

She then had an epiphany; with enough effort, she could control the blade and strike Moha. But she didn't know how to manage her ability, would this even work or would Moha snap out of his shock and kill her. She needed to try. She focused all her energy on turning the blade.

Move, move, move! Suddenly, the blade turned slowly, away from Astrid. *Yes! Just a little more... Come on!* As she clenched her fists tightly, the blade continued to turn and was now facing Moha.

Upon seeing this, Moha finally began to move, but instead of approaching Astrid, he began to back away in confusion and fear.

"No." He breathed, his dark eyes doubling in size. "No, you can't do this! You belong to me! I am the Opress! I am a god! *The* God! You obey *me!*" His voice was breaking from terror, realizing that control had shifted.

"You are not a God and will never be a God. " Astrid

called out. "Not now, not ever!"

Tacama told her of this, he told her that she could help people with this ability and now was her chance. Once and for all she could bring an end to Moha and the 'Opress'.

The dagger suddenly shot through the air at great speed.

"You obey me, Ast...!" Moha screamed at the top of his lungs but his words were cut short. The blade plunged deep into his chest, throwing him onto his back. He hit the limestone bricks with such brute force, Astrid could have sworn she heard his bones crack.

Her heartbeat calmed a little, she unclenched her fists and she breathed out. She made an attempt to walk toward Moha but her vision was shaking. A dark cloud made its way around her field of site and soon her limbs felt as heavy as obelisks.

Astrid looked at herself and checked if she had been injured. Suddenly, her entire body fell backwards and she toppled onto the sand. She was quickly greeted by a black abyss.

Thank You...

Astrid woke and found herself standing in a dark cave that reminded her much of the Tolico pyramid. Torches were lined along the walls and something churned in the distance, beyond the darkness.

"Who's there?" Astrid called out, gripping her fists.

"Do not be afraid, young princess," came a gentle voice. Suddenly, a woman emerged from the shadows and she was carrying a little baby that was wrapped snuggly in her arms. Behind the woman and her baby, their followed hundreds of men, women and children, all sharing the same eye color – blue.

"Am I dead?" Astrid murmured, her chest aching from the thought. She couldn't have just fought a war and died the second it ended.

The young woman chuckled and shook her head. "Oh no, dear," she said gently, "You are not dead. This is all an illusion, I promise, you will wake soon. Tell me, do you know who we are?"

Astrid thought for a moment. This place was so much like the Tolico pyramid but that was the only idea that came to mind. Something caught Astrid's attention, something that all of the people had in common and it wasn't their eyes. They were all wearing necklaces and they glistened like stars.

Stars... *That's it!* Astrid looked up at the ceiling to see hundreds of glowing pendants Tacama had hung there. However, as she looked, she saw no light above her.

"You're all of the people that Moha has killed," Astrid

said quietly as she looked back at them. The woman nodded and a sad smile came upon her lips.

"Yes we are," she whispered. "We came to thank you Astrid. We have been avenged, thanks to you. We are no longer the victims of Moha's deranged massacres. We can finally rest in peace. You have taught both Tolico and Egypt that we were real people. You are such a brave soul for defending people you never knew or met. You are a true leader, Astrid, and may the gods forever bless you. Thank you."

The Reign of a New Pharaoh

"What are we going to do? There is no one to continue the reign of the pharaoh!" Seth yelled, his voice breaking with concern. "The prince never lived long enough to speak, let alone know how to rule a kingdom!" He glanced over at Ray who sat beside Astrid's bed and brushed her hand gently over her hair.

"Then we must find a king. Our prince has died, along with his parents. It is not as though another son can be birthed… There's not much else we can do…"

Through what seemed like a heavy blanket that had been slowly suffocating her, Astrid finally found the muffled noise of two people. *Where am I?*

"From what country? What would they think?"

It was Seth, he was barking out curses like a wild dog. She recognized Ray who was running a wet cloth along Astrid's forehead. She wondered if this is what dying felt like. A thick blanket that completely consumes and suffocates you, no matter how much you struggle you cannot break free and before you knew it, it dragged you away.

Perhaps this was what dying was like, because to Astrid, her life seemed like something that was lying just out of her grasp. She could think and feel, but speaking and hearing seemed too difficult. She thought for a moment about the people who died in the attack.

Did they feel this way? Astrid hoped not. Gods knew what those people felt; lying out in the harsh heat of Ra's rays, each breath harder to take in than the one before it. She wondered if her mother and father felt like this as well. And what of Hitomi and the others? Had she come all this way just to die? Astrid felt as though she had failed everyone, for all she knew, they were all dead.

"Seth... are you even sure Astrid could handle something like that? Marriage seems like a big step for her. She hasn't been the type of person who would agree to any kind of rules, let alone marriage." Ray muttered, shifting uncomfortably.

Marriage? Astrid thought. *Oh gods no!* There was something she had to do. She had to wake up and say no, that she disagrees with it completely. She needed to grasp onto something, anything. Even though her consciousness seemed like something impossible to hold, she clawed her way toward it in the hope that maybe, just maybe, she could wake up.

"It doesn't matter if she wants to or not Ray, sometimes we have to do things that we don't want to and that includes..."

Astrid shot straight up in her bed and started screaming at the top of her lungs. She wasn't able to say anything, so screaming seemed to be the next best option.

"Astrid!" They yelled in unison.

Ray grabbed Astrid's arms and gently pushed her back against the bed.

"Your majesty, are you alright?" Seth asked in a worried voice.

"Alright?" Astrid gasped, "of course I'm not alright! Now tell me what's going on." She willingly lay back and took a deep breath. Perhaps it was her anger that gave her enough energy to speak but Astrid didn't care.

"I am not marrying anybody Seth, and that's final."

"Now your majesty, please give it some thought, give yourself some time to rest before you do anything rash..."

Seth paused and took a step away from the bed, his face looked petrified as he placed his hands behind his back and straightened. Astrid furrowed her brows, wondering why his demeanor had changed.

"Seth, I think you should let our princess have time to rest before she makes her decision."

Astrid turned towards the door where Xoco stood and with such a look of anger on her face that it could have rivaled her mother's scowl. She had her arms crossed, her head cocked to one side and a glare that could kill an army.

"Y-yes ma'am…" Seth said, taking another step back. The corner of Xoco's lips turned upright as she gave a slight approving nod. Finally, she looked over at Astrid and her harsh look faded.

"Are you alright dear?" She asked, walking to Astrid's bed. "I was worried about you."

"I'm fine, really." Astrid muttered. "Well, I am now." Xoco smiled gently, her smile also reminded Astrid of her mother, filled with kindness and love. Something finally hit her at last, within Xoco's gentle motherly smile was a harsh reminder. It seemed like Astrid had somehow managed to forget about it, and for a second, she didn't believe. But it was in Xoco's smile that Astrid remembered that her mother was dead.

It had only taken a moment for it to hit her. She wanted to cry but she knew that there was no time for mourning. She understood that she needed to fight to rule over her country, but it took a while for her to comprehend the fact that both of her parents were no more. She was an orphan and she felt completely alone. She then thought about the others: Hitomi, Tepin, Tacama, where were they? Where was Moha? Was what she had seen been just a dream or was Moha really dead? All of a sudden, the last few days hit Astrid hard like a rock.

"Astrid?"

Astrid shook her head in an effort to push her thoughts away. As soon as she spoke, she felt like she was reciting a speech that had been written for her, almost waiting for her. She shoved her pain away, ignoring every plea of her aching body she sat up, her voice was the only thing that remained strong. "Xoco, I need to take the throne in place of my parents."

The three of them were taken by surprise and they stared blankly at Astrid, as if she had just spoken gibberish. Seth finally spoke, "Your majesty, women can't take the throne."

"She can and she will," said Xoco sternly. Her pale eyes fell from Astrid to the floor, realizing that this young girl who was frightened to death in Tolico was becoming a strong young woman.

"She's the heir and it is her choice to either rule this country or find a husband to rule it for her." Xoco turned towards Seth and let out a deep breath. "And from the last two days, do you really expect the people to willingly take some man from a different country to rule their kingdom? Or would they want the young woman who saved them from a monster? Tell me boy, who would you choose?"

Seth's jaw dropped and a deafening silence spread across the room.

"I…" he whispered, looking from his feet to Astrid. "I would choose our princess…" With the help of Ray Astrid stood.

"Good." She said before looking at Xoco. Astrid's expression soon changed as she asked Seth a serious question, "Now tell me… who died?"

Xoco seemed speechless but realized that Astrid was growing stronger by the second. Astrid would now become the new pharaoh of Egypt. Xoco noticed that Astrid spoke differently too; her voice deepened slightly and in spite of her obvious pain, she stood straight and strong.

"Xoco?" Astrid asked once more, "Tell me I can handle it."

"Y-your parents…" Xoco looked at Ray and Seth, almost as if she was looking for permission. Both of them looked down at the floor in an effort to avoid her gaze. Xoco let out a sigh and balled her fingers into fists.

"Your parents, your brother and Cacama, one thousand and eighty-three citizens died, including the Karnak priest, and… and Moha…" Astrid felt her muscles tighten and her stomach churned.

Moha did die then, she thought, *but how? He survived last time.* She wanted to ask but she could see that Xoco was hurt from simply speaking his name. Astrid had almost forgotten for a moment that Moha was her son. *How could I possibly ask Xoco how he died?* But she needed to know. Summoning up courage, she turned to Seth.

"How was Moha killed?" She muttered, hoping that Xoco wouldn't hear.

"You don't remember?" Ray interjected.

"I remember something but I need to know if it's true."

Xoco nodded gently and said in a stern tone, "You killed him Astrid. It's hard to explain but… you did it."

Something stirred in Astrid's stomach, something she had never felt before. It was somewhat like relief but she was more confused than ever. It took her a while to realize that she had actually killed someone. Then she felt remorse; she had no right to take his life away, no matter how evil he was but his death prevented the slaughter of more innocent people.

"Astrid?" She looked up at Xoco, noticing that she had been silent for a while.

"Good." Astrid muttered. "Good, I'm glad."

Out of nowhere, Tacama barged into the room, his eyes aflame with anxiety.

"Astrid?" He yelled, shocked to see her up and awake.

"What happened? No, I don't care what happened; I know what you did. That was so stupid. What were you thinking? Do you know how worried we've all been? You've been asleep for three days. Three days!"

Despite her weakened state, Astrid still managed to let out a whole-hearted laugh.

"There's a fine line between stupidity and bravery, remember? Or in my case, between bravery and unconsciousness."

Tacama let out a heavy breath and rushed to her side; embracing her tightly in his arms. "I'm just glad that you're alive."

Then Tepin joined them and from the corner of her eye, Astrid saw Hitomi, leaning on both a cane and against the doorway, she was just as bruised and swollen as Astrid, but she was smiling as brightly as ever.

"Glad to see that you're up twinkle toes."

Astrid coughed through a giggle. "Twinkle toes? What kind of nickname is that?"

Hitomi rolled her eyes, "You should have seen yourself out there, you were like a great dancer, so take that nickname with pride."

Xoco gently clasped a hand on Astrid's sore shoulder and kissed the top of her head.

"I'm sorry dear, but Astrid has a new nickname, she's to be known now as the pharaoh of Egypt."

The coronation was not to be held outside in the historical location where hundreds of pharaohs had been given their rightful title. While a new throne room was being constructed for the new pharaoh, Astrid's father's throne room had been turned into the new coronation room. But people began to wonder what had happened to the last one, the one that had been used for hundreds of years.

Astrid tried to put aside her feelings about the massacre,

but she had let herself slip for a moment. She refused to allow anyone near the coronation site. She wouldn't even let the families retrieve their loved ones. No one asked questions though; they thought it unwise to question her authority. She only informed Seth that she would be the only one allowed into the site. Not even Hitomi, Xoco or Tacama could enter. The only way anyone would be able to see it was from Astrid's room. The balcony outside of Astrid's room looked over the ruins and all its gore. Throughout the entire night on the eve of her coronation, she stood on the balcony until the hot sand soaked up the blood and Ra began to steal whatever life was left in the victims, leaving them shriveled and lifeless. It was a reminder to Astrid alone, to never let something like this happen again, even if it cost her own life.

Later that night however, one person was able to recognize her grief most of all. Tacama, who had seen the massacre of his entire family shared her pain and refused to let her dwell in her own suffering. He stayed with her until dawn, telling her stories about great adventures and the people he and his father met when he was just a boy. He reassured her of her heroism and her courage.

"Unfortunately, life lessons come at a price, yours came at the price of innocent lives but you've learned a lot. Lessons make a good king, trust me." He took her Azuli sword from the stand beside him and extending its blade pointed to the inscription that had left Astrid curious since the beginning. "You know what this says?" He asked.

She shook her head. He took her hand in his and placed the hilt on her palm.

"The Azori king gave this to my father in battle. They had made a deal to fight the war to the death. That, Astrid, is what that inscription means. It's also one of the main reasons I gave this to you. No matter what happens, I will always be beside you. We'll be together as allies and as friends - no, as family. To the death."

He smiled and placed a kiss on her head. "And with that said, I think both of these kings need some sleep." Tacama made an attempt to leave, but just for one moment since the massacre, Astrid let down her guard.

"Tacama…" she whispered softly and that's all she had to say. Tacama knew how much pain she must have been feeling. She told him she couldn't be alone, not with all the memories and words that were swimming inside her mind, and he recognized that. He sat down beside her and wrapped a blanket around her shoulders.

Tacama could never have raised his son but for a moment, as he sat beside Astrid with her head upon his lap, sleeping soundly for once, he finally felt for a brief moment that he was a parent; or at least a much older brother.

Upon a throne of silver, bronze and gold that once belonged to Thutamun, Pharaoh of Egypt, there now sat the young princess Astrid. She did her best to stay still with her head held high and her shoulders back, staring at the crowds of people who were all watching her. In the front row were Xoco and Hitomi alongside Tepin and Tacama who smiled and gave her a nod of approval.

Just a few hours before this moment Tacama had come into her room to make sure she was all right and when he parted he simply said, "You'll be great out there."

Now she sat on the throne that once belonged to her father, sitting in front of thousands of her father's people, her people. She had to keep reminding herself of that. She was no longer just a princess, she was pharaoh. She wondered if it was meant to be this frightening.

The experience was uncomfortable; she was dressed in a white skirt and her developing breasts were held tight against her chest by a white linen binding strip. Gods, what she would give to take off these silly clothes and put on something comfortable. The only thing about these clothes that was remotely familiar to her own attire was a gold cape that was pinned to the back of her bandeau. For some reason, that one piece of fabric made her feel more like herself in this odd situation. She had worn a cape like this almost every day in Egypt.

Even if she did ask for this, it didn't make her any less nervous. Everyone was staring at her; some with smiles, others with disgust. Not to mention the re-occurring thought that maybe what happened at Hitomi's coronation would happen again, it appeared that most of the gathering were thinking the same thing as most of them were slightly nervous.

"The upper and lower halves of our country…"

Astrid finally snapped out of her train of thought and saw a shadow hanging above her. She glanced up to see the inside of her father's war crown. He had never worn it, so in a way, it felt like it was made just for her. In any other case, she would have been adorned with the double crowns of upper and lower Egypt but her people were the ones who requested a warrior king be crowned with the blue circlet of war itself. It was scary to think that her people saw her as a warrior. She was no longer a rebellious little girl with childish fantasies and an unknown future, she was now a soldier… a killer.

The crown was bigger than she remembered and it made her even more nervous than before.

"Will be united…"

Oh Gods… she thought, *this is it…*

"Under one pharaoh…"

What if I'm not as good as my father? The crown was inching closer towards her head. *What if I fail?*

"Under the name given by our gods is our pharaoh, Hatshepsut Astrid."

The priest lowered the crown onto Astrid's head and to

her surprise, it was a perfect fit. She was Hatshepsut Astrid, Pharaoh of Egypt. No more running away, no more being scared. Although she still looked like a young woman with pretty jewelry and makeup, along with a crown that sat upon a head of braids, her people no longer saw her as a fifteen year old. They saw her the way she looked during battle; clothes ripped, makeup gone, jewelry strewn and a weapon in each hand. She couldn't run away, she couldn't afford to be afraid, she had to stand and fight, to prove herself to her father's people. Her people.

And she would, she would protect her people and her country… to the death.

The Space Between

There were rumors that the young prince Moha had a lover who was once a concubine of his father's. This was a lie of course; even if Moha had a lover, he wouldn't have chosen a concubine. He would, however, choose a whore from the streets, but that didn't happen till the rumors had long ceased and Moha had taken the throne of Tolico.

Her name was Lilith, a beautiful woman who looked like a goddess among the dirty peasants. She didn't look like anything from this realm, from her elegant appearance to the silk that cloaked her curvaceous body like liquid gold. She had hair the color of wheat and eyes the color of the sun. Moha didn't know where she came from or why she looked the way she did, but he didn't care either way. She was a thing of pure beauty, a sliver of opulence among filth, a true diamond in the rough.

Lilith was vastly different to any other being that had ever lived on Moha's tiny island. Moha believed that people who possessed ocean blue eyes were granted godly abilities, but he was wrong. It appeared that Lilith had also been blessed by the gods. While the men and women Moha sacrificed for his own selfish desires had the abilities of the earth, Lilith had the ability to bring back the lives of the dead. However, with every life she resurrected, another soul had to be sent into the underworld in its place.

Lilith sighed, folding her arms as she walked across and exited the room. Suddenly, the hem of her golden dress was stained with blood. In noticing a blood trail, she followed it across the sticky crimson floor until she came to its source. It was Moha and he had a long deep gash in the center of his chest. A look of shock and pure unadulterated horror stained his cold face. Lilith went onto her knees and placed her delicate fingers over the wound.

"You finally got yourself killed?" She laughed under her breath, scratching her long nails deep into the wound. She felt the tiny shards of his shattered sternum and gently pushed them aside before her fingertips slipped over Moha's ruptured heart.

She rolled her eyes, squeezing it softly, saying, "I'd rather not kill someone else just to bring you back."

She pulled out her hand and wiped it on one of the only clean spots of Moha's kilt. "But I guess that's what I'll have to do. Gods Moha, you could have avoided this but no, you had to get yourself into more trouble."

She stood and brushed her hair away from her face before leaving the house. She said out loud with a sigh, "Why do I love such an insolent ass?"

She returned shortly afterward, carrying a heavy sack behind her. Fortunately, the house that Moha stayed in at times was in a place where Lilith wouldn't have to worry about prying eyes. She threw the sack down beside Moha's cold corpse and untied it, revealing the near-dead body of an old woman.

"You owe me Moha." She growled, wiping sweat from her brow. "My dress is ruined thanks to you."

Teasing a dead man wasn't exactly out of character for her. Besides, yelling at Moha when he returned to life would just make him angry and no one would want him angry, not even his lover.

The Day of Moha's Death

Moha's body was burned in a pyre and the men responsible for the disposable of his corpse were long gone. Out in the desert and away from the curiosity of people, Lilith emerged. Her skin glistened palely in the moonlight and her sharp topaz eyes glared at the smoking remains of her lover.

"Once again, you've got yourself killed. When is this nonsense going to stop, my love? At this rate you'll end up staying dead for good. You understand that, don't you?"

She slipped off the long blue dress that covered her voluptuous figure from Ra's hot rays, to reveal nothing more than a pale silky slip.

"I'm not ruining my dress with your blood and gore again Moha." Lilith knelt down, once again unfolding a heavy sack to pull out the unconscious form of a dying man taken from the massacre. She grabbed a knife that was strapped to her thigh and used it to slit the man's throat. She stood, balancing his blood on the blade before trickling it onto Moha's charred body. Energy surged through her veins and she closed her large eyes as she took in a deep breath and held it there. She stretched back her neck, reaching for her ability deep within her soul. She found it at last and exhaled heavily.

With the release of her breath came the gasp of another. She opened her eyes and stepped back, wiping the dirtied blade on her undergarment. After a moment, she looked at her lover who was gasping for breath. Lilith rolled her eyes and put the dagger back in its place.

"Do you have to act like such a drama queen?" She scoffed. "Get up Moha, you can't die yet, you still have work to do."

She grabbed her dress and pulled it back on, carelessly glancing at Moha. He finally gathered his senses and sat up in his fully regenerated body. He sighed deeply, his breath still labored and he looked up at Lilith.

She gave him a sly grin and outstretched her hand, saying softly, "You owe me one again, my love."

No one ever knew Lilith, apart from those who occasionally scrounged enough money to sleep with her. She lurked in the space between love and hatred for Moha, waiting for him, waiting to do whatever he asked of her. She was his most loyal companion. She didn't need recognition for her deeds; all she needed was him. At least, what he had to offer.

Acknowledgments

I began writing Pyramids when I was twelve years old. The idea I had in my head was that I wanted a princess to save herself. Soon, I realized as I stared at the sloppy handwriting that this was impossible. No one can truly save themselves. Humans can be as brave as they want, but we all thrive on interactions, introvert or extrovert. Besides, how could a weak little girl save herself from a crazed maniac like Moha? She couldn't. On the other hand I didn't want Astrid to be saved by some handsome prince. As a young teen, I thrived on science fiction, especially Star Wars, I lived and breathed those movies like food and air. Finally, I noticed something while I was watching them. Luke Skywalker was a young man, just as Astrid was a young woman, the two of them wanted to fight a war but they were too weak to do so. So, they got help. Both Luke and Astrid needed inspiration, a will to fight, something close to heart. Love.

No, no, no, I thought. Now when I first thought of this book, I didn't want romance. But then I realized that love wasn't just between a romantic couple. It is a strong bond between two people, like Luke Skywalker and Han Solo, or Obi Wan Kenobi and Anakin Skywalker. Friendship to me was the strongest love that my young mind could fathom. And you know what? It still is to me. That's where Hitomi came in. Now at first, Hitomi was weaker than Astrid.

For a college assignment, I had to read and research *The Hero With A Thousand Faces* by Joseph Campbell. I realized that in every story there was the hero, the sidekick, and most of all, the mysterious 'Supernatural Aid'. I didn't like this idea, it worked well for Star Wars but it just didn't feel right as I tried to write my story like that. It was just *wrong*.

This is where my second inspiration came in. When I was about fourteen or so, I started watching an Australian sci-fi show called Farscape. This show basically looked at Joseph Campbell's theories in storytelling and spat in its face. Now this I liked. A band of misfits joining together for the same cause. Totally different personalities, different kinds of love, different kinds of goals in life. Yes, this was perfect. This is what I wanted to do with my life; I wanted to write something like that. So, I sort of did and then my story came alive. I breathed life into a story and gave it a heart, a brain, and a purpose.

I always had this band of misfits in mind but now, it was fueled by love, friendship, and a cause. I had 'The Coward', 'The Old Woman', 'The Fool', and lastly, 'The Runaway'. (I just made that up, but it works!).

I know this page is supposed to be dedicated to loved ones and friends and I'm getting there, I promise. But with every good story, there has to be a back-story right? Exactly. So…

In the beginning, Astrid was the lead character and everyone else, just sidekicks. But of course, with this 'band of misfits', I realized that their relationship had to change – no, I needed it to change. It was as though my story had called out to me from a word document, screaming "Save me, fix me!" So instead of a feeble old woman and her secret son, a girl who lived in the forest, and a kidnapped princess, I had to develop their characters into something better, something stronger.

Now, I can get to the 'thank you' part. Kind of.

So, in the process of editing and rewriting my book, it was four o'clock in the morning, Christmas Eve. I'm sitting on my couch, hunched over my laptop, head in hands and

I'm groaning, "How do I make her better!" I spent six days staring at one line: the introduction of Hitomi. How could a little girl live in the forest? How could she just befriend this runaway based on the fact that they shared the same eye color? She couldn't of course. She spent most of her life in the forest alone, with only sporadic visits by Xoco who brought food, clothes and bedding.

Then I realized something, Hitomi had lost everything precious to her. Sure, that had been made clear before in the story but now it hit me. She lost her family, her country, her freedom. She lived in an old shack in the middle of the forest, a shack that once belonged to an old drunk, and she was unable to see anyone other than an old woman once a month. She must have been so quiet, so guarded from others. That's when I started to connect to Hitomi in a way that I wasn't able to before. She lost everything she ever loved, and she was beginning to love Astrid as a friend and maybe as a sister. They shared the same goal and they shared the same fear of King Moha. Hitomi knew that Astrid could possibly die. She didn't want to love or even speak to anyone in fear of growing close to them and then losing them. I shared that fear as well. This is why.

Fast-forward about six months. My novel is almost edited, it is once again, extremely late at night and I am hunched over my laptop with my head in my hands, groaning, again. But it wasn't over a fictional character, but over a page like this. I had read hundreds of thank you friends and thank you mom and dad in dedication pages but I shared the same fear Hitomi did. What if I put someone's name in this book and then regretted it later, hating it every time I saw my book in stores, knowing that his or her name was somewhere in its pages.

Then I thought, well, maybe a name really isn't that important at all. Maybe what's important is the love connected to the label "friend". Now I can use this page properly. I'd like to thank my best friends. The ones that have been with me for years, that probably grew sick and tired of every rant about my characters day in and day out. The ones who were truly there for me and inspired me. They were the Astrids to my Hitomi, they gave me hope and they made me happy.

However, there will be a name in here, the name of someone who was fitted into my dedication page. I explained that I dedicate my work to you, my readers, I explained how my life was saved by a movie saga and how I wanted to repay the debt to the readers of my books. That's what I wanted my dedication page to be, ever since I was thirteen years old. That changed though, just a little of course. I wanted to thank my aunt. So I will.

Thank you Victoria, thank you for listening to me blabber about characters, to hear about this book until the day you died. Thank you for inspiring me and encouraging me to write. Thank you for reading scenes even though your vision was failing. And thanks for putting up with the groans of your niece while she hit the keyboard in a fit of writer's block while you were trying to sleep.

You guys are probably confused, so let me explain. My aunt was like Xoco to Astrid. She would tear apart worlds for the people she loved and would equally slap them for saying something stupid. My aunt looked like the most perfect angel and she was, but she was also a demon to the people who deserved her wrath. My aunt was like a mom to me, she was the most perfect person one could ever imagine. She completed my world. My aunt died June 30th 2013 from cancer, she passed in her sleep while her daughter and nieces were a little tipsy (and I was half high on Benadryl due to my cat allergy) and laughed about some unimportant joke until we were on our knees and bright red.

That is what my aunt loved most in the world, she loved

laughter and her family, just like Xoco. So, sure, I dedicate this book to my fans that take my stories to heart but I also dedicate this to my aunt. My best friend, my angel, my protector, my knight in shining armor, destroyer of ignorant jerks and greatest person to ever have lived.

Mum, you'll never be able to read this, but in some way, you'll know that I have included this in my story. I just want to say thank you, I love you, and if there is a heaven and you are there, give them hell! You'll forever be my Xoco to my Astrid and I will always love you to the death – and a long while after that.

And finally, the very last person I'd like to thank is... you. I have yet to know you, and you have yet to know me but I thank you anyway because you took some time out of your schedule to read this book.

Maybe you saw a review on-line or maybe you thought it was interesting and thought of checking it out. Maybe you saw it at a library or were forced into reading it by a friend. Whatever it was, I'd just like to thank you. I know it's weird for some chick in a book to address you as "you" and you probably think I'm talking about everyone and not just you. In a way I am, which I admit is quite strange but honestly, I am just thanking you for picking this up and taking the time to read even the first sentence. It makes the long nights of writing, blaring music, hanging from trees and staring at the sky for a glint of inspiration so worth it. So thank you reader, thank you.